SHADOW GUARDIAN

MEETS PUSS AND BOOTS

SHADOW GUARDIAN SERIES

SHADOW GUARDIAN
MEETS PUSS AND BOOTS

ROBERT J. LEWIS

4 Horsemen
Publications, Inc.

4 Horsemen
Publications, Inc.

Published By: 4 Horsemen Publications, Inc.

4 Horsemen Publications, Inc.
PO Box 417
Sylva, NC 28779
4horsemenpublications.com
info@4horsemenpublications.com

Edited by Jen Paquette

Library of Congress Control Number: 2024947900

Paperback ISBN-13: 979-8-8232-0695-2
Hardcover ISBN-13: 979-8-8232-0696-9
Audiobook ISBN-13: 979-8-8232-0698-3
Ebook ISBN-13: 979-8-8232-0697-6

This book, as all my books, is dedicated to my beloved mother and father, Dolores C. Lewis and Robert O. Lewis. I also dedicate this to my brother Harry Lewis who doesn't miss an opportunity to brag about my writing to his friends. This is also dedicated to the diva Bonita, who took me for plenty of mini walks and demanded plenty of snuggles and attention while writing this.

To my Bonita Boys, Randy, Chris, William, Berto, Rodney, Brian, and Kalvin, and my Diva Duo, Amanda and Donna, for all the love and support they have given me over the years. To Tyda Surge for making me smile when I needed it and being one of my biggest cheerleaders.

A special dedication to my editor Kris Cotter for making me a better writer and all her enthusiasm for my writing. I know I'm sending her a manuscript that I am certain is error free, but we all know THAT ISN'T THE CASE.

U

TABLE OF CONTENTS

PROLOGUE

COVERED IN A SHEEN OF SWEAT and dirt, Joshua stepped into the log cabin. Chest heaving from his training, he watched Jack busily crushing herbs and roots. There was no telling if it was for dinner, medicine for Teddy, or both. He knew Teddy was resting in the bedroom, wrapped in mystical healing leaves to undo whatever the Demon Twink and his minions did.

"He's awake if you want to see him," Jack said without turning around. "The forest said you did good."

Jack's connection to the plants still amazed Joshua. "Tell them thank you for such a good workout." Joshua fidgeted in the doorway. "I should get cleaned up first."

"Joshua, we need to talk." Jack set down his mortar and pestle before turning around. His face was full of regret. "I can't help you and your friends. I have obligations and responsibilities here. I can't leave the forest right now. You know that, right?"

Hurt, Joshua argued, "You left the forest to find Teddy. Remember? When you kicked me out of the forest and abandoned me."

"Joshua, you know I didn't abandon you. We talked about that." Jack moved to Joshua's side. "You weren't ready and you were so full of anger. You would have gotten hurt or worse if you'd gone with me."

Joshua felt the pain of truth in Jack's words. "It still hurts," Joshua confessed. "Why can't you leave the forest?"

"News of the Demon Twink has spread as well as my attack on his facility." Jack ran a soothing hand along Joshua's arm. "Mysticals are flooding the forest, seeking sanctuary and protection."

Joshua looked knowingly into his eyes. "You have to protect them, like I have to help Aspen find Gaymer."

"And protect Morgan City." Both men turned to see Teddy holding himself up in the doorway. "Your life is there, not here."

Joshua looked at Teddy with imploring eyes. "But I love you." He looked at Jack. "Both of you."

"We love you too," Jack reassured him.

Teddy came over to them on unsteady legs. "You'll always have a home here with us. You'll always be my Sugar Bear, and I'll always be your Teddy Bear."

"And I'll always be your Plant Daddy." Jack pulled them both into a hug.

Joshua returned the embrace. "I don't want to leave you. I just got you both back."

"We'll be here when you come back." Teddy squeezed them. "Go help your friends."

Jack nuzzled them. "Don't worry about us. I'll nurse Teddy back to health, and there's a forest full of Mysticals ready to lend a hand to help protect the forest."

"Here, take this." Teddy pulled away. He pulled a gold necklace with a gold medallion on it from his pocket. "Wear it always. It'll protect you."

Joshua took the jewelry and examined it. There was a sword on one side of the medallion and a shield on the other side. "I can't take this. It's yours."

"Take it. It will make sure you come back to us." Teddy took the necklace from Joshua and put it over his head. "I mean it—wear it always. Understand?"

Joshua nodded. "I will."

"Good, now go get cleaned up. You stink," Teddy teased.

Jack glared sternly at Teddy. "And you need to get back to bed. Those healing leaves won't work if you don't let them."

"I'm tired of being in bed all the time," Teddy grumbled.

Jack pointed to the bedroom. "Go on. I'll bring you something to eat in a little while."

Jack waited until he was certain that Joshua was in the bath cleaning up before he brought Teddy his soup. Setting the bowl on the night-stand, he waved a hand over a napping Teddy. The leaves glowed blue, telling Jack everything he needed to know about Teddy's vitals.

Teddy opened his eyes and smiled. "I'm going to miss him."

"Me too." Jack sat on the edge of the bed. "Do you think that medallion the old woman gave you is going to protect him?"

Teddy shook his head. "I don't know. I hope so. Did you guide that creature from the labora-tory through the forest and into the city like she instructed you to?"

"I did. It took some creativity to do it, but I managed to steer it out of the forest into the city." Jack put his hand on Teddy's. "I wish we could have helped it."

Teddy sat up in the bed. "We don't have the resources to help it. She said it would find the help it needs in the city."

"Dante! Please! Let me out of here!" Finn cried out from the confines of his bottle. "I'm sorry! I did everything I could! I swear!"

Petting the white furry dog in his lap, Doctor Gingerman groaned. "Can't you shut him up?"

"I could, but I love how his pleas taste in my ears." Dante's delighted smile turned to a frown when he heard the white dog growling. "Fine." Peering into the bottle, Dante soothingly addressed Finn. "Baby, be quiet while we have our meeting, and I will forgo the rest of your punishment."

Sitting in the center of the bottle prison, naked and clutching his knees to his chest, Finn looked up at Dante's giant eye. "I promise I did everything I could."

"I know you did, baby, but failure must be punished," Dante explained in a loving voice. "Be my good boy. Stay quiet during our meeting, and I'll release you after we finish."

Hopefully, Finn asked, "Promise?"

"Promise," Dante answered with a wink. Returning his attention to Doctor Gingerman, he asked sarcastically, "Happy?"

Doctor Gingerman gave him a sardonic grin. "Very. Thank you."

"Now, back to business." Dante sat back, spreading his thin body out over the plush loveseat. "How is Gaymer working out?"

Doctor Gingerman petted the white dog in his lap. "It has taken some time, but he's finally accepted the fact he isn't going anywhere. He's been able to perfect the hypnotic device." He shot his eyes to the bottle. "Unfortunately, your boy failed to prevent Teddy and Experiment B12 from escaping."

"My husband," Dante corrected him firmly. "Teddy was useless. Whatever that Drus did to him prevented the Rage Seed from taking root in him. B12 was a loss, but we can create another."

The dog in Doctor Gingerman's lap growled. "B12 was a success because I created a serum using Teddy's blood. It prevented the Rage Seed from overpowering it while still giving it the special abilities. It's what I used to stabilize Papa Bear and Honey Bear and that foolish lab assistant who stole one of the Build and Burn doses."

"Darn it." Dante yawned, bored. "The Drus has fortified his forest, and more Mysticals are taking up refuge there every day. There's no way we can get Teddy out now."

Petting the dog, Doctor Gingerman said, "The tracker in B12 shows he's in Morgan City. I have unfinished business there. I can take the Three Bears with me to retrieve B12. We need to test their new stable states anyway."

"What about that hero Lip-Sync was fighting?" Everyone's eyes turned to Finn's voice shouting from the bottle. "Wasn't he after Lip-Sync because she kidnapped Teddy? Couldn't we use him to lure Teddy out of the forest?"

Dante smiled. He gingerly ran a hand along the length of the bottle. "I believe my husband has redeemed himself."

"Take Lip-Sync and Death Drop and capture him," Doctor Gingerman ordered. "Finn can stay and protect our assets here."

Dante cut his eyes at Doctor Gingerman. "Don't give me orders."

"Those orders come from the Chairman of the Board." Doctor Gingerman stared Dante down.

Dante nodded in acquiescence. "Understood." He ran a hand along Finn's bottle. "We'll have to settle for Death Drop. Lip-Sync is on vacation." Dante stood, carefully picking up Finn's bottle. "Now, if you'll excuse me, I'd like to reward my husband for his idea."

"Demons." Doctor Gingerman stood with the dog and went to leave the room.

Dante corrected him. "Demon Twinks."

Aspen sat beside the prison hospital bed that Doug Trainer occupied. He hated the man who slumbered with his hands wrapped in bandages for allowing the Demon Twink to take Gaymer. He also felt sorry for him, being separated from the man he loved with no hope of ever seeing him again once he was sentenced for his crimes.

"You don't need to come see me every day," Doug said without opening his eyes.

The air around Aspen grew cold. He did his best to keep the bitterness out of his voice. "I do it for Gaymer, not you."

"You do it for you," Doug said, opening his eyes and looking at Aspen. "Have you been able to locate Gaymer yet?"

Aspen's eyes flashed silver then blue. "No. We think the Demon Twink is hiding him in a pocket dimension. We're waiting for someone to return to help locate him."

"When you find him, and you will, tell him I'm sorry and that I love him." Remorse filled Doug's voice.

Aspen carefully put his hand on Doug's bandaged hand. "You can tell him yourself after we rescue him." The chill in the air left. "Diego and Alex came up with an idea to give you use of your hands back. They have a team working on it right now."

"I don't deserve it," Doug admitted solemnly.

"No, you don't." Aspen stood. "I won't be able to come visit for a while. Juan Carlos pulled some strings to have someone else visit you."

Doug shook his head. "I don't deserve visitors."

"You don't, but you're getting them anyway," Aspen said coldly before leaving.

CHAPTER 1

"THERE'S STILL NO SIGN OF OUR thief. Maybe they took the night off," Sentry reported over the coms as he zoomed over the River Side skyline on his Shadow Disc.

"Like you should be?" Aiden scolded with love. "You've been back four days and done four patrols. We're a team, Sentry. You don't have to do it all yourself."

Seeing movement on a rooftop, Sentry set his disc to hoover. "I'm not trying to do it all, Shadow Voice. I'm giving you guys a break. I was gone for three weeks." Sentry watched the lithe figure make impossible leaps from one rooftop to another. "I think I have them."

"Calling in backup," Aiden announced.

Sentry saw a flashing light coming from the rooftop. "Wait. I think they are signaling me."

"It could be a trap," Aiden warned.

Sentry guided the disc down. "Only one way to find out." He stepped off the disc to the rooftop. "Stay ready." Sentry scanned the darkened rooftop. "Whoever it was is gone now." Sentry waited for a response. "Shadow Voice?" Sentry tapped his ear piece. "Shadow Voice, are you there?"

"Hello, cutie." Lip-Sync stepped out from the shadows. "I hope you don't mind. I wanted a private conversation with you." She held up a glowing white crystal. "This will shield us from prying eyes and eavesdroppers."

Sentry took his discs from his sides and stood ready to hurl them. "What do you want?"

"You," Lip-Sync answered sultrily. She sashayed toward Sentry. "It took you long enough to find me. I was debating whether to rob a bank next."

Sentry ordered, "Stay where you are." She held up her hands in supplication. "What do you want, Lip-Sync? What are you doing here?"

"I told you. You." Lip-Sync winked at him. "I missed you."

Sentry scowled at her. "Tell me where Gaymer is."

"That I cannot do even if I wanted to. Demon assassin code." Lip-Sync twirled some of her black hair with her fingers. "Besides, I don't know."

building. "Everything I stole is over there, sweet cheeks." She did a backflip off the building.

It took Sentry a moment to realize Aiden was screaming in his ear. "Sentry! Are you there?! If you can hear me, I'm activating Lobo and Siren!"

"No, I'm okay," Sentry answered calmly. He opened the envelope and read the name of the restaurant and time on the paper inside. "I found all the stolen goods."

Flabbergasted, Aiden asked, "What happened? I lost contact with you."

"I think I got asked out on a date." Sentry put the paper into one of his side pockets.

"Oh," Aiden paused. "What are you going to wear?"

Joshua barely had his Shadow Disc landed in the command center before Aiden pounced on him for details. "Okay, dish, bitch."

"There's nothing to dish," Joshua said, stepping off the disc and pulling off his domino mask. "Lip-Sync claims she was committing the crimes to get my attention so she could ask me out."

Aiden's eyes went wide with delight. "How strangely romantic." The tips of Aiden's hair ignited as he excitedly peppered Joshua with questions. "When is the date? Where is it at? What are you going to wear? Do you think it's a trap? Should we be on standby in case it is? How are we doing your hair and nails? Do you think you'll go to her place, or are you bringing her back to ours?"

"Aiden, your hair is on fire," Joshua said casually as he started tugging off his uniform.

Aiden's eyes went up to look at his hair. "Again?" Aiden closed his eyes in concentration. The flames snuffed out. "That's one way to deal with split ends." Aiden's face brightened again. "Okay, so what are you wearing? Do you want me to design something for you?"

"Did the Shadow Patrol find all the stolen goods?" Joshua asked, ignoring the question and slipping on a t-shirt.

Aiden pursed his lips. His hair ignited again. "Yes. Now why are you avoiding my question?"

"Because I'm not going." Joshua stripped out of his pants then slipped into a pair of sleep pants. He looked at Aiden and said, "Hair."

Aiden looked up at his hair and sighed. "Again? I swear. Ever since I went supernova, that's been happening more and more." Aiden closed his eyes and extinguished the flames. "Why aren't you going?"

"I have two men in the forest who I love and love me." Joshua moved to one of the plush chairs they recently added to the command center and sat down with a groan. "Besides, it's probably a trap."

Aiden plopped down cross-legged on the floor in front of him. "Aren't you in some sort of polyamorous relationship?"

"No." Joshua shook his head. "Maybe? Possibly? We haven't had a chance to define our relationship yet."

Aiden threw up his hands in frustration. "Then what can it hurt? Go!"

"It could be a trap," Joshua argued, tossing the note to Aiden.

Reading the note, Aiden rolled his eyes. "Why go to all the trouble of asking you out to a restaurant to set a trap when she could have tried to trap you on the rooftop?"

"Will you stop making sense?" Joshua huffed.

Aiden rocked in excitement. Sparks of flame crackled and popped around him. "Okay, that's a fancy restaurant. Diego is actually banned from it." Aiden tapped his finger on his chin. "You can wear your black dress pants that show off your, um," Aiden winked at Joshua, "curves and your royal blue dress shirt with a red tie."

"With my uniform underneath in case Lip-Sync tries to slice me with one of her fans?" Joshua asked sarcastically.

The sparks around Aiden stopped. "Diego and Alex will be back in the morning from their vacation. Diego and Freddy can keep an eye on you on your date if you want."

"No, don't do that." Joshua chewed his lower lip. "I'll go but don't tell anyone. Especially Aspen."

Aiden scrunched up his face. "Yeah, they may ruin your date by trying to capture Lip-Sync."

"Let's go to bed." Joshua stood up. "You have work in the morning."

Aiden jumped up and winked at him. "And you have a date to prepare for that you're not going on."

CHAPTER 2

FROM HIS FIRE ESCAPE, KEAGAN watched one of the city heroes zooming away overhead. He waited until the hero was gone before he reached back into his apartment and picked up his messenger bag. Slinging it across his shoulder, he grabbed the railing. Jumping over, he leapfrogged his way down with the grace of a cat until he was on the ground.

Kneeling down, Keagan opened the messenger bag and pulled out a tiny kitten. "Okay, time to do your thing. I know our stray is here. Now lure him out." He set the kitten down.

The kitten let out a dutiful "Meow," then started walking down the alleyway, its tiny tail whipping about.

"Come on. I know you're there." Keagan's pupils elongated to cat eyes. "Come on. You like the kitten." Keagan saw movement in the darkness of some trash cans. The kitten sat down and looked at the same place Keagan was looking. His words came out a purr, "Yes, pet my little kitty."

The kitten let out a beckoning "Meow."

The young man wrapped in a dirty lab coat that Keagan had been leaving food out for cautiously crawled out from behind the trash cans. He looked over at Keagan briefly before skirting over to the kitten and gently starting to pet it. The young man smiled merrily.

"Yes, he's a cute kitty," Keagan purred softly.

Careful not to spook the young man, he slowly crawled toward them. He paused when the young man looked at him. It looked as though the young man was about to run, but the kitten stood and began rubbing up against him, running in and out his legs to the young man's delight.

"Such a good kitten." Keagan started moving slowly toward the young man.

He stopped when he was about a foot away from the young man. He didn't notice Keagan because he was preoccupied petting the kitten. Slowly, Kegan opened up the messenger bag and pulled out a cloth napkin that he delicately placed on the ground. He then reached in and pulled out a peanut butter sandwich and a bottle of water. He set them down on the tiny cloth square.

Sitting cross-legged on the ground, Keagan decided to make himself known. "Fierce really likes you." The young man's head darted up to look at Keagan. There was a look of fear and confusion on his face. "The kitten." Keagan pointed to it. "His name is Fierce." Keagan pointed to himself. "I'm Keagan. Who are you?"

The young man looked at Keagan in confusion. "Do you not talk?" Keagan asked.

"Meow," Fierce answered.

Befuddled, Keagan questioned the kitten's answer. "He can but doesn't know how to?"

"Meow." Fierce took hold of the young man's sleeve and tugged him toward Keagan.

Keagan rolled his eyes at the kitten. "Hey, I'm trying. It's taken us this long just to get me this close." Fierce tugged the young man toward Keagan until they were an arm's length away. Keagan picked up the sandwich and held it out to the young man. "For you."

Fierce let go of the young man's sleeve and began grooming himself. The young man stared at the sandwich. He looked at Keagan briefly, then snatched the sandwich away. He sniffed it, then shoved most of it into his mouth, devouring it in a matter of seconds.

"Here." Kegan pulled out another sandwich. He held it out for him. The young man hesitated

11

a moment, then he snatched that sandwich too. "Fierce tells me he sees you out here during the day scavenging for food." The young man paused chewing to look at him questioningly. Keagan pointed at the kitten. "Fierce. He's my guardian."

Confused, the young man cocked his head to the side. "Never mind." Keagan thought for a moment. "I need to figure out a way to communicate with him."

Fierce let out an impatient "Meow."

"I know you were told I have to help him, but I have to figure out how to talk to him first," Keagan snapped. "Why don't you ask him if he wants to come back to my apartment?"

Fierce looked up at the young man. He cocked his head at the kitten. Fierce looked back to Keagan and let out a smug "Meow."

"Well, great, he'll come back to my apartment, but how am I—" Keagan narrowed his eyes at the kitten. "Why didn't you tell me you can communicate with him?"

Fierce let out another smug "Meow," then started rubbing up against the young man.

"Why couldn't I have been given a better guardian?" Keagan took the water bottle, cracked it open, and handed it to the young man.

When the young man took the bottle, his and Keagan's fingers touched. Images flashed in

Keagan's head. The young man awakening in a tube filled with some greenish yellow liquid. Then of the young man strapped to a table, screaming in pain as a faceless scientist injected him with something. The young man admiring the shiny boots of a guard. The guard laughing when the boot connected with the young man's head. The young man curled in a ball in nothing more than his underwear being beaten and kicked by the guards.

An explosion and the young man escaping into the woods. The young man, cold and hungry with only his boots and lab coat for protection. Food and water mysteriously appearing for him. The forest seemingly guiding him out and toward the city. The loud noises. The strange people. Feeling hungry. The cute kitten and then Keagan handing him a sandwich.

"Did you really go through all that?" His heart hurting for what the young man went through, Keagan pulled back his hand.

The young man stared intently at Keagan. He worked his jaw like something was stuck to the roof of his mouth. "Ye—yes," he managed to force out in a deep gentle voice.

"You spoke!" a wide-eyed Keagan exclaimed. "How?"

The young man tapped the fingertips of his other hand together. "The touch." He struggled to form the words. He looked at Keagan. "People were mean to you. You saved Fierce. You died."

"Sort of, yes." Keagan scratched his head. "That's how I got Fierce as a guardian."

Fierce let out a cheery "Meow."

"What do you mean: it worked?" the young man asked the kitten.

Keagan glared at the kitten. "Yeah, what do you mean it worked?"

Fierce let out a reluctant "Meow."

"You could have told me touching him would help him learn how to talk," Keagan snapped, putting the small napkin back in his bag. To the young man, he asked, "What's your name?"

He shook his head. "I don't have one.'"

"Meow," Fierce chimed in merrily.

Keagan glared at the kitten. "Not funny."

"I like it." The young man beamed. "Boots like the boots I like."

Keagan grabbed Fierce and held him up to look him in the eyes. "You're not funny."

"Why is it funny?" Boots asked curiously.

Keagan sat Fierce down. "He calls me Puss. Together, we're Puss and Boots."

"We're together?" Boots asked smiling, cocking his head to the side.

Keagan stood up and held his hand out. "No, we're not together." Boots took his hand and stood up. The lab coat came open, allowing Keagan to see his toned muscular chest that tapered down into a perfect V to his tight green briefs. Keagan managed to choke out, "We're um, friends."

"Friends." Boots smiled, closing his lab coat. "I've never had a friend before."

Keagan scooped up Fierce and put him on his shoulder. "He's not getting up the same way we got down." He looked up at his fifth floor apartment. "I guess we're using the stairs." He took Boots' hand. "Come on. Try not to make any noise. I have nosey neighbors and you're," Keagan looked Boots up and down, "not exactly dressed."

"Okay." Boots smiled.

With the quietness of a cat, Keagan led Boots into the building. Stealthily, they climbed the stairs, Boots holding Keagan's hand. Keagan snuck glances at Boots. The young man was grinning merrily and his mocha brown skin glowed with happiness.

Arriving at his door, Keagan announced, "We're here." He looked down at their joined hands. "I sort of need that hand."

"Oh, I'm sorry." Boots blushed, letting go of Keagan's hand. "I like holding your hand."

Blushing, Keagan pulled his hand away. "It's okay." Pulling out his keys, Kegan fumbled with the door. "It's not much, but it beats the streets."

"Meow," Fierce agreed.

"I'm saving up to get a nicer place," Keagan said, stepping into his tiny one-bedroom apartment. "This is the kitchen, living room, and bedroom." Pointing to the one door, he said, "That's the bathroom. You can freshen up there."

Boots looked about the apartment in awe. "This place is so nice."

"Why don't you get out of those dirty clothes and take a shower?" Keagan went to his second-hand dresser and started rummaging through his clothes. "I might have some clothes that fit you." He grabbed a t-shirt and gray sweatpants. Turning around, he said, "These will do for—" Keagan's eyes bulged when he saw Boots standing there naked. He quickly turned back around. Flustered, he said, "You're naked."

Confused, Boots responded, "You said get out of my clothes."

"Meow," Fierce confirmed, jumping up onto the dresser.

Keagan glared at the pompous kitten. "I know what I said. Will you take him into the bathroom and help him get cleaned up?"

"Meow." Fierce jumped onto his cat tree, then made his way down to the floor.

Keagan held the clothes behind him. "I know you're naked under your fur, but that's different."

"Did I do something wrong?" Boots asked, taking the clothes from Keagan.

Keagan shook his head. "No, you're just a little bit more comfortable with your body than I'm accustomed to."

"I'm sorry. I'm not used to privacy," Boots responded with a shrug. "I was always being watched. Even when I bathed."

Keagan swallowed hard. He was having lustful thoughts toward his guest. "Well, you'll have your privacy here. Well, to an extent."

"Okay, so you're not going to watch me in the shower. Got it," Boots said before Keagan heard the bathroom door shut.

Keagan turned around to see Fierce grinning at him. Annoyed, Keagan said, "What?"

"Meow," Fierce answered with a smug grin.

"Right. Where is he going to sleep?" Keagan's eyes went wide. "I'm going to have to share my bed with him."

"Meow," Fierce snickered.

Keagan shot the kitten a dirty look. "No, there will not be any funny business going on."

CHAPTER 3

SNUGGLING ON THE COUCH WITH his head resting on Diego's chest, Alex asked sleepily, "Why exactly was I so against letting you take me on vacation?"

"Because you were being a dick," Diego joked, moving his hand to brush over the freshly shaven sides of Alex's scalp, then up to run through his perfectly trimmed hair on top. "I really like your new haircut."

Alex playfully thumped Diego's chest. "I had to get it because of the suit outfit my boyfriend designed for me to wear."

"Hey, Alegro came up with the original design. I only," Diego's voice went deep and sultry, "improved upon it."

Alex pecked Diego on the cheek. "The only action it and all that training Freddy put me through will see is in the bedroom."

"Why don't you go out with me on patrol tonight?" Diego suggested.

Alex shifted so he could look to see Diego's face. "You're serious."

"Yes." Diego shifted them so he lay on top of Alex. "You have to use those skills to keep them sharp."

Alex laughed. "I'm not going out on patrol with you." Alex ran a hand up Diego's broad back. "My place is in Shadow Command."

"You wanted to be my sidekick before." Diego ground his hips into Alex. "You could be Shadow Boy."

Alex burst out in laughter. "No."

"You're really good with a bo staff, and you're a surprisingly good dancer." Diego thought for a minute. "How about Pole Dancer?"

Alex quickly shot out, "Absolutely not!"

"Yeah, I realized it when I said it." Diego chuckled. "Maybe something computer oriented like Hard Drive, or what was the news calling you? Whiplash?"

Alex shook his head. "No and no."

"Then you come up with a name." Diego kissed him lightly on the lips. "Something that inspires fear in the criminal underbelly."

Alex chewed his lower lip. "Hhmm, how about High Tech?"

"I like it." Diego grinned at him. "I like this better, Shadow Paladin. That way everyone knows you're with me."

Alex playfully teased Diego, "Jealous much?"

"No," Diego pouted, "and that guy was flirting with you at the resort."

Alex hugged Diego close. "Doesn't matter if he was or wasn't. I'm all yours." Alex pecked Diego on the lips. "It's going to be High Tech."

"Fine," Diego said, pretending to be disappointed. "You know, we should get dinner started. Juan Carlos said he wants a big dinner to celebrate Felipe's first day as mayor and Esmerelda and Gato's return."

Alex whined, "It's only eight in the morning. Why do we have to start so early?"

"Did you forget we have to feed Freddy?" Diego asked, pulling them up to a sitting position.

Alex groaned. "You know, for a wolf, he really makes a *cochino* of himself."

"Look at you speaking Spanish," Diego gushed. Patting Alex's leg, he said, "Come on. Juan Carlos said he left detailed instructions for us."

Alex allowed himself to be pulled up by Diego. "I wonder how Felipe's morning is going."

Keagan sat rigidly on the other side of the desk from the newly elected mayor, Filipe Montoya. This was his first official day in office. That meant changes were coming. Inevitable changes, like staffing. He was the last remnant of Mayor Trainer's vanguard. That meant it was finally his time.

"Keagan, I know you've noticed that everyone that worked under Mayor Trainer is gone from these offices," Mayor Montoya said formally. "Aside from you."

Refusing to draw the painful conversation out, Keagan jumped in. "So do you want me out now? The end of the day? Do you want me to stay long enough to train my replacement?" Boldly, Keagan added, "Spit it out or does a cat have your tongue?"

"None of the above," Mayor Montoya answered, startled. "I was going to ask you if you'd stay on. With a substantial raise, of course." Keagan sat there stunned as he continued, "My father and I reviewed your work history here, and after some extensive background checks, we're convinced you had nothing to do with the former Mayor Trainer's Pup attack."

Offended, Keagan snapped, "Of course not. I hate dogs."

"Yes, well," Mayor Montoya cleared his throat, "I believe in paying people their worth. Since you've been invaluable in this transition," he pushed a folded piece of paper to Keagan, "I was hoping this would be enough to keep you with me."

Keagan couldn't hide the Cheshire cat grin that spread across his face. "I'd have taken it for half this amount."

"I would have paid you double that if I could," Mayor Montoya offered with a smile. "It also comes with a benefit that would be sort of a favor for me."

Keagan raised an eyebrow. "I thought you were straight."

"What? I am." Mayor Montoya thought for a moment. "Wait. Did you think? No! No! No! I wasn't suggesting that! Why would you think I was suggesting that?!"

Keagan shrugged. "You said it was a benefit and a favor for you. I put two and two together and got that you wanted me to—"

"Stop!" Mayor Montoya held up his hand. "I know you live in the industrial district. I was going to offer you a place in North Side. My brother's boyfriend's old apartment. They moved in together, but my brother's boyfriend still keeps some of his stuff there. I'm tired of hearing them fight about it. If you move in, then my brother's boyfriend has to get his stuff out. Are you interested? The rent is real cheap."

Keagan mentally debated it. It wasn't South Side or River Side, but it was a step up from the Industrial Area. "Maybe. Do they allow pets? I have a kitten."

"They sure do." Mayor Montoya smiled with relief. "There's plenty of room. You could even get a roommate if you wanted. I can call the building manager now. He's my brother's brother."

Keagan cocked his head curiously. "Your brother is the building manager?"

"Oh, no. He's my brother's brother, not my brother. He's sort of my uncle." Mayor Montoya thought about it for a moment. "Yeah, he's my uncle." Seeing the confusion on Keagan's face, Mayor Montoya laughed. "We're not blood related. We're related by love. Juan Carlos is my actual father. Diego, my brother, was raised by him. He grew up with Freddy, and they are like brothers. To me, he's like a fun uncle."

Keagan shook his head. "Please tell me your family tree forks out and not in."

"Very much so." Mayor Montoya laughed. "You know how it is having family and having people you love like family."

Keagan shrugged. "No, not really. I was an orphan."

"I'm sorry. I knew that too. Forgive me, please," Mayor Montoya apologized. "Let me make it up to you. We're having a family dinner to celebrate my first day. Why don't you join us? You can take off early, go home, and freshen up then go see the apartment and come over with Freddy and his boyfriend, Salvador."

Nervously, Keagan tried to decline. "I couldn't. I couldn't take an apartment without Fierce looking at it too."

"Fierce? Is that your boyfriend?" Mayor Montoya asked.

Keagan chuckled. "No. Fierce is my kitten."

"Bring him along. Gato will love him." Mayor Montoya thought for a moment. "I'm not sure what he is. Maybe a cousin?"

Keagan tried to deflect again. "I couldn't leave Boots at home by himself."

"Is Boots another cat? Bring him along," Mayor Montoya quickly responded.

Anxiously, Keagan said, "No, he's not a cat. He's, um..."

"Your boyfriend?" Mayor Montoya asked.

Keagan shook his head. "No, he's someone I, um..."

"You make him sound like a stray you picked up off the street." Mayor Montoya laughed.

Keagan grimaced. "He sort of is. He's staying with me for a while."

"Well, bring him along too." Mayor Montoya slapped the desk. "It's settled. You'll go home at three, get ready, go see the apartment, and then come to dinner. I'll even arrange for a car service for you."

Feeling no way out of it, Keagan reluctantly said, "Okay."

"Great. I'll call my dad and let him know there will be two and a kitten more for dinner." Mayor Montoya pulled out his cell phone. "He must be in a meeting. I got his voicemail."

Juan Carlos and Dion sat in her office in silence. After several awkward moments, they both blurted out, "Thank God, Diego comes back tomorrow." They both burst out into laughter.

"If you ever tell him I said that..." Dion grinned, leaving the threat unfinished.

Amused, Juan Carlos responded, "Your secret is safe with me. I assume mine is safe with you."

25

"Things have been quiet. Efficiency is up." Dion slumped back in her chair. "Not a single fire to put out."

Juan Carlos added, "It's been boring. Creativity is down. Even Doctor Tyson asked when Diego would be coming back."

"Odd how he went from not being able to be around Diego to them being best work buddies." Dion thought for a moment. "Do you think Aiden had anything to do with that?"

Juan Carlos groaned. "Aiden. His hair keeps igniting. I'm surprised he hasn't set off the fire alarms yet."

"I'll take flaming hair over a walking blizzard," Dion huffed. "If I want hot coffee, I have to get it myself. Aspen keeps freezing everything."

Juan Carlos nodded. "We haven't had a chance to study their powers, but I think their powers are tied to their emotions."

"It makes sense. Demona says her powers are tied to her emotions." Dion grinned. "I am grateful for that."

Juan Carlos winked at her. "I bet you are. Are you ever going to thank Diego for setting you two up?"

"I gave him Doctor Tyson for his special projects. I think that is thanks enough." Dion sighed.

"He seems to be really happy there. I hear he loves his lab assistants."

Juan Carlos smiled proudly. "My grandbaby loves working with him. Alegro says they have learned a lot from him."

"Alegro spoke?" Dion questioned.

Juan Carlos winked at her again. "Sort of. Chitter translated."

"Chitter. I love that little robotic squirrel." Dion shook her head. "I think they are the only being that can get Aspen to smile."

Steel filled Juan Carlos's voice when he said, "We'll get Gaymer back for him and put an end to this Demon Twink threat. I promise."

"I hope so. The tracking device went dead before you could mobilize to save him. Demona hasn't even heard a whisper of where he might be." Dion's voice had a hint of defeat in it. "Wherever he is, I hope he's safe."

CHAPTER 4

GAYMER STOOD READY AT THE open unguarded door. It was the first step in his escape plan: get out of the workshop prison the Demon Twink held him captive in. Then it was on to step two, which he would figure out once step one was a success.

This time it's going to work, Gaymer told himself. He took a deep breath, closed his eyes, and ran at the deceptively simple door, stopping only when he was sure he was through. "Fuck!" he exclaimed when he opened his eyes to see he was still in the workshop.

"Language." Dante's condescending voice came from behind him. Gaymer turned hate-filled eyes on the Demon Twink. He stood on the other side of the cursed door with someone Gaymer did not know. "I would think by now you'd have learned there is no escape."

Gritting his teeth, Gaymer snarled, "I'll get out of here, and when I do, Ice and I will make you pay."

"Oh, you poor delusional soul." Dante stepped through the doorway with his companion. "Allow me to introduce you to my husband, Finn." The young man beside Dante nodded. "Finn, this is the troublesome Gaymer."

Finn smiled wickedly. "I've heard so much about you."

"All bad, I hope." Gaymer crossed his arms over his chest defiantly. "What do you two twinks want?"

Annoyed, Dante ranted, "Demon Twinks. Seriously? How hard is it to put the word demon in front of twink? It's not that hard. Demon Twink. See how easy it is to say that? Demon Twink."

"Is he serious right now?" Gaymer asked Finn.

Finn shrugged. "What can I say? He's proud to be a demon twink."

"Fine." Mockingly, Gaymer repeated his question, "What do you two *demon* twinks want?"

Dante grinned. "Thank you. Now for the matter at hand. Where are you on the hypnosis project?"

"The computers with the project are over there." Gaymer pointed behind him. "I'm right here." He pointed at himself. "Do you need to know where anything else is?" Gaymer answered sarcastically.

Dante twisted his hand in the air, activating the bracelet on his wrist. Gaymer fell to his knees in pain. When the torture faded, Gaymer turned venomous eyes on Dante. "I told you I won't work with you. I'd rather die."

Finn criticized his husband. "Three weeks and all you've been able to do is get the pocket twink to hate you?"

"Do you want to go back in your bottle?" Dante threatened, eyes flashing red.

Finn's voice went apologetic. "I didn't mean it like that. You know how I get when I've been denied your attention for so long."

Three weeks?! Gaymer thought, standing back up. *He's had me in here for three weeks?! I thought it was three days!*

The red in Dante's eyes faded. "I forgive you. I'm a little on edge because I haven't been able to give you attention," his eyes flashed red as he flicked his wrist, sending Gaymer crumpling to the floor in agony, "and this one seems to take special pleasure in annoying me."

"Perhaps you should allow me." Finn put his hand Dante's wrist, releasing Gaymer from the torture. "You don't spend centuries as a rat without learning how to get what you want from humans."

Dante warned him, "Do not fail me again, my love. I've grown rather fond of you. I would hate to have to replace you."

"I won't fail. I know what is at stake." Finn kissed Dante. When their lips parted, red swirls of magical energy flowed between them. "Go. I've got this."

Dante ran his hand through Finn's short hair. Fisting his hair roughly, Dante snarled, "Do not fail me again." Releasing Finn's hair, Dante exited through the door that taunted Gaymer.

"How can you be with someone like that?" Gaymer asked, struggling to get up.

With a nefarious smirk, Finn asked, "Someone that has a vision? Someone that is ambitious? Driven? Determined?"

"Someone who is mad with power. Someone who is cruel and evil," Gaymer countered, using a nearby table to hold himself up.

Finn fluttered his hand in the air. "Isn't that the pot calling the kettle black?"

"What does that mean?" Gaymer spat out.

Finn scoffed. "At least he knows he's evil and cruel. You hold on to some sanctimonious idea that you're good, when your cruelty and evil rivals that of Dante."

"You're crazy!" Gaymer shouted back angrily.

Finn snapped his fingers. A clouded mirror set in blackened embossed carved wood appeared. "Shall we review the tape, as they say? I think a little self-reflection is what you need. It's time you stopped living in your make-believe world and faced reality."

"You're the one living in a make-believe world if you think you're going to make me think I'm anything but good," Gaymer snapped, finally able to steady himself on his own feet.

Finn waved his hand, sending the clouded mirror to float in front of Gaymer. "Let us clear the smoke from the mirror and see." The smoke in the mirror cleared, letting Gaymer see himself. "Remember when your parents died? When your uncle told you what happened?"

The image in the mirror changed to a young Gaymer looking up at his Uncle Doug Trainer. His uncle was crying. Gaymer was shaking his head. His uncle tried to hug him, but young Gaymer pushed him away. Young Gaymer mouthed the words, "I hate you," right before he started pummeling his tiny fists against his uncle's chest.

"That was the start of your cruelty toward your uncle." Finn waved his hand, turning the mirror into a collage of Gaymer yelling or arguing with his uncle. "All he wanted was to love you, to connect with you. You were his only family, and you pushed him away at every chance."

Finn waved his hand. The mirror clouded over in smoke, then dissipated to reveal scenes of a young Gaymer yelling and throwing things at Brutus. "Brutus loved your uncle. He tried to be your friend. You hated him for that and tried to drive him away because you wanted to punish your uncle for surviving."

"That's not true!" Gaymer shouted at the mirror. Guiltily, he admitted, "I tried to drive him away because I was jealous he had my uncle's affection."

Finn waved his hand again. The mirror clouded over, then cleared to show Gaymer at his computer. "You wanted to win his love. Is that why you helped him steal all that money?" Finn waved his hand again. The scene changed to Gaymer working on the hypnosis boxes. "Or why you improved the hypnosis boxes?" Finn waved his hand again. Gaymer was working on the electro pulse guns. "Or you created the guns?"

Finn snapped his fingers. The image morphed into Ice being shot. "The same guns that shot Ice." Finn clouded the mirror with a wave of his hand. It revealed Gaymer working on his uncle's gloves. "Let's not forget those wonderful gloves you made for your uncle." Finn snapped his fingers. Gaymer watched in horror as the gloves malfunctioned, disfiguring his uncle's hands. "Did you sabotage them like you did those guns?"

"Are they okay?" Gaymer asked, voice breaking and tears streaming down his cheeks.

Finn waved his hand. The mirror filled with smoke then rolled out to reveal Aspen, sitting rigid at his desk. His blond hair sparkled blue with ice crystals and his rosy cheeks were as white as snow. "Your harlot? Yes. I guess. They've grown a bit cold from what I heard."

Finn waved his hand, revealing Doug Trainer laying alone in the hospital bed, hands bandaged. "Your uncle? Not so much. There's nothing really they can do for his hands. He's lying alone in a prison hospital bed, awaiting his trial." Finn waved his hand, causing the mirror to vanish. "See? You're evil and cruel as well. You just tell yourself that you're not."

"I want to see them," Gaymer demanded. "Now."

Finn laughed sinisterly. "I just showed them to you."

"You know what I mean," Gaymer snarled.

Finn studied Gaymer. Seriously, he said, "Wording does matter. Remember that." He stared intensely at Gaymer. "Fix the programming in the hypnosis boxes like Dante wants, and

I will reunite you with your family. I'll even throw in fixing your uncle as an added incentive."

"What's the catch?" Gaymer asked suspiciously.

Finn snickered. "Making a deal with a demon. See? You are evil."

"What's the catch?" Gaymer repeated, crossing his arms.

Finn smiled deviously. "I will reunite you with your uncle and his fiancé Brutus. Call me a sucker for love."

"What aren't you telling me?" Gaymer wiped a tear from his eye. "Wording matters. Remember?"

Finn smiled proudly. "You're a quick learner." He waved his hand about. "Of course, we'll bring your uncle and fiancé here. They are facing major prison time after all."

"No deal," Gaymer said through gritted teeth.

Sarcastically, Finn asked, "What would you have me do? Magically make all their charges disappear? Make their failed attempt to take over Morgan City suddenly not happen?"

"I want our freedom," Gaymer responded. "I don't care how you do it, but make it happen."

Finn waved his hand flippantly. "Fine. I'll make it happen somehow."

"Deal." Gaymer stuck out his hand.

Taking his hand, Finn said, "Deal."

"Any luck with our guest?" Doctor Gingerman asked when Dante returned.

Plopping down onto a couch, Dante growled, "Finn is handling it." Seeing Death Drop holding Finn's bottle up and staring into it with one eye, Dante snapped angrily, " Unless you want to end up in a bottle like that one, I suggest you leave my husband's bottle alone!"

Death Drop jerked her head to see the angry Dante. Her eyes darted left and right. She smiled guiltily before carefully placing the bottle back down. Giving Dante a toothy grin, she stood straight with her arms behind her back. She took two side steps away from the bottle.

"Of all the times for Lip-Sync to take a vacation," Dante groaned. "Are the bears ready for their part of the plan?"

Doctor Gingerman spoke with pride. "Yes. My new and improved Three Bears have been armed with the state-of-the-art weaponry I designed."

"Then I say we move ahead with our plans. We need B12 to move on with our plans." Dante caught Death Drop inching toward Finn's bottle. He waved his hand from left to right, sending her flying across the room and crashing into the wall. "Good help is so hard to find."

Doctor Gingerman watched Death Drop comically fall backward onto her back with a thud. "Are you sure this one is up for the task? We need Joshua alive."

"I'll be there with her." Dante rolled his eyes at Death Drop twisting her head straight. "Take the bears, find B12, and I'll..." Dante paused. He smiled. "Finn did it. Gaymer's on board."

Curiously, Doctor Gingerman asked, "How?"

"By offering him something he couldn't resist." Dante let out a diabolical laugh. Spotting Death Drop tiptoeing toward Finn's bottle, he waved his hand again, sending her back into the wall. Death Drop fell onto her face. Dante groaned. "If you weren't Lip-Sync's protégé, I'd banish you back to the nether realms."

Doctor Gingerman stood. "We'll leave in the morning." He looked down in derision at Death Drop who had rolled over, black Xs over her eyes, her hands folded over chest with a single wilting flower in her hand. "Seriously, you couldn't hire someone a bit more professional?"

"She was part of a buy one get one free deal." Dante shrugged. "You get what you don't pay for."

CHAPTER 5

JUAN CARLOS PATTED DIEGO ON the back. "Everything smells wonderful. Who did you hire to cook it?"

"Hey!" Alex exclaimed, offended. "I'll have you know we cooked everything except the bread. We went to the," Alex searched for the word, "pana ... der ... re ... ia." He put the word together proudly. *"Panaderia."*

Juan Carlos smiled at Alex. "Your Spanish is getting better, and I apologize. I was only teasing." Juan Carlos inhaled deeply. "You can smell the love in the food."

"I hope we made enough." Diego lifted the lid of a pot to check on the simmering corn.

Puzzled, Juan Carlos said, "Felipe only invited two people. The recipes I left can feed twenty people." Laughing, he shook his head. "Freddy."

"Freddy," Diego repeated, "and his wolf metabolism."

Juan Carlos looked around. "Speaking of which, where is Freddy? I figured he'd be in here trying to steal food."

"He's outside with Chitter and Alegro," Diego answered with a smirk.

Alex covered his mouth to hide his amusement. "They're playing fetch."

Juan Carlos did his best to refrain from laughing. "You know, I've caught him running around the garden with Chitter and Alegro on his back."

"He really is taking his *tío* responsibilities seriously," Diego said with a chuckle.

Juan Carlos then asked, "Where is Salvador? With the boys downstairs?"

"No." Pouting, Alex slumped against the wall. "He's showing my apartment to your son's guests."

Diego rolled his eyes. "You haven't been back there since we moved most of your stuff out. You live here now, baby daddy."

"No!" Alex blurted when he saw the look in Diego's face.

Diego grinned. "Come on."

"What?" Juan Carlos looked between the two.

Alex repeated adamantly, "No."

"What?" Juan Carlos asked again, a little annoyed.

Unamused, Alex said, "My code name is not going to be Baby Daddy."

"I, uh," Juan Carlos began, trying not to burst into laughter, "should check on the boys."

Alex shouted at Juan Carlos's retreating back, "It's not funny!"

"No, it's not." Diego pulled Alex into his arms. He tightened his grip before adding, "It's hilarious!"

They heard Juan Carlos exclaim from the living room, "Felipe! How was your first day?!"

"You're safe for now." Alex hugged Diego back. "Too many witnesses."

Diego gave him a slight squeeze. "You can punish me later. Let's go see everyone."

"Okay." Alex pulled away. Smirking, he said, "You called me your daddy."

Diego stammered, "Hey! Wait! I did not!"

"Yes, you did!" Alex rushed out of the kitchen.

Chasing after Alex, Diego shouted, "I did not call you my daddy!" Tackling Alex, they landed on one of the couches with Diego on top. "Now who is the daddy?"

"Me!" Alex laughed. His laughter stopped when he heard the creak and then snap of wood.

Alex managed an "Uh oh" right before the couch crashed to the floor.

Stunned, Felipe asked, "Is this a sex thing?"

"With these two, I honestly don't know anymore," Juan Carlos answered with a shake of his head.

Untangling himself from Alex, Diego explained, "He said I called him my daddy!"

"You did call me your baby daddy!" Alex argued, getting up from the collapsed couch.

Looking at Felipe, Juan Carlos said, "I still don't know."

"It's not a sex thing," Diego huffed.

Alex grinned. "Well, it sort of is."

Felipe sighed. "Can we be normal when Keagan and his friend get here?"

"You ask for the impossible," Esmerelda answered, gliding into the room with Gato on her arm. "Who is Keagan?"

"Esmeralda!" Juan Carlos exclaimed, rushing over to hug her. Kissing her on both cheeks, he said, "I've missed you!"

Gato teased, "What about me?"

"I missed you," Diego said, pulling Gato into a bear hug.

"Keagan is my personal assistant," Felipe said, hugging Esmeralda and kissing her on both cheeks. "It's so good to see you again."

Hugging Felipe, Gato asked, "Is it safe to bring people who aren't in the know?"

"He'll find out eventually. Better to gauge him now." Alex kissed Esmeralda on both cheeks, then did the same to Gato. "I'm happy to see you both."

Pointing at the broken couch, Esmerelda asked, "Dare I ask?"

"He said he was my daddy!" Diego blurted.

Crossing his arms, Alex defended, "You did call me your baby daddy."

"No fair, using my words against me," Diego argued.

Raising an eyebrow, Gato asked, "Is this a sex thing?"

"No!" Alex snapped.

Diego hip bumped Alex. Playfully, he said, "It sort of is."

"Enough!" Esmerelda held up her hand. With a swirl of her wrist, the couch reassembled itself. "That will last until morning. Now no more daddy talk, or I'll give you both a tail." She saw the impish looks Diego and Alex shared. "Don't test me, boys. Now where are Freddy and Salvador?"

Diego pointed to the rooftop garden. "Freddy's playing with Chitter and Alegro."

"Salvador is showing my apartment," Alex grumbled.

Juan Carlos sighed. "Boy, get over it. You live here now."

"Fine." Alex smiled. He put his arms around Diego. "Everything I love is here, anyway."

Esmerelda covered her face with her hand. "Must everything with you two be so dramatic?"

"Yes," Diego and Alex answered, grinning at each other.

Kissing Gato on the cheek, Esmerelda said, "I'm going outside to see Freddy and meet the niblings before I banish these two to a Hell dimension or turn them into something horrible."

"I'll get us something cold to drink then join you." Gato patted her arm.

Juan Carlos ushered them into the living room. "Good idea, Gato. I think we all need a drink after that."

"How was your first day?" Alex asked, carefully sitting down on the magically repaired couch.

Felipe shook his head. "I don't know how Mayor Trainer was able to run the city and found time to be a criminal mastermind. If it weren't for Keagan, I'd probably still be there."

"Then he's working out? Good." Juan Carlos patted his son's leg. "I knew that skittish boy on the screen couldn't be part of the Puppy Pack."

Felipe laughed. "Skittish? He's anything but skittish,"

"Virgin mojitos all around," Gato announced, carrying a tray of bubbling glasses garnished with mint and lime.

"Thank you." Juan Carlos took one of the glasses. "What do you mean he's not skittish? Everyone I interviewed said he was timid and quiet. He would jump at any loud sound."

Felipe took one of the glasses. "I don't know what to tell you. He's confident. Assertive." Felipe squeezed the lime into the glass. "He does have a weird habit of purposely knocking things off his desk."

"The party can start now! I'm here!" Aiden announced, gliding into the room. His red-tipped hair ignited as he twirled for everyone.

Alex pointed at his head. "Hair."

"Again?" Aiden groaned in dismay.

Shooting a blast of cold at his brother's hair, Aspen said, "Got it." Steam rose from Aiden's hair. "Will you get your powers under control already?"

"You're one to talk, Miss Chill," Aiden sniped back. "You bring a cold front everywhere you go."

Joshua put a hand on their shoulders. "Boys, keep it under control. Salvador messaged me that he was on his way up with the guests."

"I'll make more drinks." Gato disappeared into the kitchen with the tray.

Taking a seat beside Alex, Aiden whispered, "Is that the sexy and mysterious Gato?"

"I'm not mysterious!" Gato shouted from the kitchen.

Laughing at Aiden's mortified expression, Alex said, "Cat hearing, remember?"

"Aren't you with Doctor Tyson?" Diego asked curiously.

Aiden waved his hand about in dismissal. "There's no harm in window shopping."

"Really?" Diego grinned.

Alex shoulder bumped him. "There is for you."

"Everyone. Best behavior," Juan Carlos commanded, then vaguely threatened, "or else."

Salvador announced from the foyer, "We're here!"

Everyone stood to greet the newcomers. Salvador appeared first, trailed by Keagan with Fierce perched on his shoulder and a brightly smiling Boots in clothes that were two sizes too small. Seeing all eyes on them, Keagan stopped. Sensing Keagan's hesitation, Boots did as well; however, a curious Fierce leapt from Keagan's shoulder and landed gracefully on the floor.

No. No. No. Not now, Keagan thought, feeling his power emerging. He blinked and his pupils elongated. He quickly covered his eyes. He tried to stop it, but it kept surging forth. Thinking quickly, he lied, "My contact slipped. Is there a bathroom I can use? I'm so sorry."

"Down the hallway," Felipe answered, concerned. "Do you want me to take you?"

Keagan grabbed Boots' hand. "No, no. Boots can help me. Enjoy your party." Pulling Boots down the hallway, he added, "Again, I'm so sorry."

"Curious," Juan Carlos said, sitting back down.

Joining his father, Felipe added, "Yeah, because I just realized he doesn't wear contacts."

"Fresh virgin mojitos," Gato announced, carrying in a tray of drinks.

Fierce perked up and ran to block Gato's path. Sitting down, tiny tail whipping about happily, he let out a chipper "Meow."

"Who do we have here?" Gato asked, stepping around the kitten to set the tray down.

Following him, Fierce let out a proud "Meow."

"Fierce, huh?" Gato squatted down to pet the kitten. "Such a powerful name for such a tiny kitten."

Fierce let out an offended "Meow."

"I believe you." Gato laughed, petting Fierce. "You are very powerful and bigger on the inside."

Teasingly, Alex chimed in, "So is Diego."

"Hey!" Diego shouted as the others hid their laughter.

Ignoring everyone else, Fierce looked at Gato and let out a curious "Meow."

"No, they can't come out and play right now." Several of Gato's tattooed cats had emerged from the inked jungle and were prowling up and down his arms. Picking Fierce up, he stood. "Maybe later." Seeing everyone staring at him, he asked, "What?"

Diego cleared his throat. "Gato, since when can you talk to cats?"

"I can't," Gato answered, puzzled. "Why?"

Joshua pointed at Fierce. "You just had a conversation with that kitten."

"Meow," Fierce hissed.

Petting Fierce, Gato said, "You're too young to use language like that." To Joshua, he said, "His name is Fierce."

"So you can talk to Fierce?" Aspen asked, confused. "What was he saying?"

Fierce let out an annoyed "Meow."

"Language," Gato scolded the kitten. "No, he's not being a nosey bitch."

Aiden burst out into laughter, igniting his hair. "That kitten called you a bitch!"

"Hair!" everyone shouted.

Aiden closed his eyes in concentration, extinguishing the flames. "Why does that keep happening?"

"Why does what keep happening?" Esmerelda asked, cradling Chitter in her arms.

With Alegro wrapped around him, Freddy sniffed the air. "Smells like Aiden gave himself flame highlights."

"Gato, where did you get that kitten?" Esmerelda asked, carefully sitting Chitter on the end table.

Chitter cocked its head left and right. "Did we get a kitten?"

"It's Keagan's rude kitten," Aspen huffed.

Fierce let out a spiteful "Meow."

"Language," Gato scolded, then added, "Yeah, he is kind of a bitch."

Esmerelda studied Fierce in Gato's arms. "You can understand him?"

"Meow," Fierce said, annoyed.

Taken aback, Esmerelda said, "Well, excuse me."

"I told you it was rude," Aspen grumbled.

Fierce leapt from Gato's arms to the coffee table and hissed at Aspen, "Meow."

"Well, you called me a bitch," Aspen snapped back at Fierce.

Diego cleared his throat. "Do you guys really understand this kitten, or are you guys messing with me?"

"Meow," Fierce purred at Diego.

Diego gushed. "Awe, you're cute too." He thought for a moment. "Wait a minute. I just understood that kitten."

"That's because he is a guardian," Esmerelda answered. "He's projecting his thoughts into our minds."

Salvador tapped his chin in thought. "They taught me about those in Atlantis. They are supposed to guide mystical champions."

"Who is the mystical champion though?" Alex asked.

Juan Carlos shrugged. "He came here with Keagan and his friend."

"Please, don't tell me." Felipe put his face in his hands.

Sympathetically, Diego said, "It could be the kid who wears clothes tighter than mine."

CHAPTER 6

"**A**RE YOU OKAY?" BOOTS ASKED when they entered the bathroom.

Keagan shut and locked the door, then removed his hands from his eyes, revealing his oval pupils. "We need to leave. Something is triggering my power. I think we're in danger."

"Okay," Boots took Keagan's hands in his, "I'll get Fierce and we'll go."

Keagan caught himself unconsciously purring at Boots' touch before dread filled him. "We left Fierce out there!" Keagan began pacing. "We need a plan."

"This bathroom is bigger than your entire apartment," Boots marveled, looking around.

Keagan stopped mid-pace to look at Boots. He tried to be angry at the brown skinned Adonis, but the jovial innocence on his face melted Keagan's heart. "Boots, focus. We have to get Fierce and get out of here."

"We can just grab Fierce and tell them something came up," Boots said with a shrug.

Keagan shook his head. "That..." He paused. "That actually might work. We'll say I have to get my special eye drops from the apartment."

"Keagan," Boots took his hand again, "I won't let anyone harm you."

Keagan patted his cheek. "Thanks, but I can take care of myself. Besides, I'm supposed to protect you, remember?"

"Then we'll protect each other." Boots hesitantly let go of his hand. "Let's go get our kitty."

In the hall, Keagan's cat ears heard a woman's voice say, "That's because he is a guardian. He's projecting his thoughts into our minds."

"Wait," he whispered to Boots.

"They taught me about those in Atlantis. They are supposed to guide mystical champions," he heard Salvador say.

A male voice Keagan didn't recognize asked, "Who is the mystical champion though?"

"He came here with Keagan and his friend," answered a voice Keagan knew to be Juan Carlos's.

Then he heard Felipe say in dismay, "Please, don't tell me."

"It could be the kid who wears clothes tighter than mine," said a voice Keagan knew to be Diego Sanz.

Resolutely, Keagan pulled Boots along to the end of the hall. "He's my guardian."

"We, uh, have to go back to Keagan's for his butt drops," Boots stammered out nervously.

Keagan gawked at Boots. "Butt drops?! What are butt drops?! It was eye drops! And we're not doing that anymore!"

"I'm sorry. I got confused." Boots cringed. "I was looking at your butt."

Diego nudged Alex. "Good to know we're not the only couple like that."

"We're not a couple!" Keagan yelled, more fervently than he intended.

Boots scratched his head. "A couple of what?"

"Demon spawn!" Esmerelda shouted. She began twirling her hands, but Gato grabbed her by the wrists. "Gato! What are you doing?"

Confused, Gato answered, "I don't know! I'm not in control of my body!"

From Gato's tattooed arms, the stirring felines cried out in unison. Two lionesses emerged, one carrying a black wooden baton with golden and black spheres on the end while the other carried a simple black box. Landing gracefully, they went to Keagan, placed the items before him, then bowed.

"For me?" Keagan knelt down and petted the two feline queens on their heads. "What are they?"

Diego jumped up from the couch. "Alegro, get Juan Carlos and Felipe to safety!" He touched the center of his chest, activating his suit. As the microbots formed his suit around him, Diego ordered, "Everyone else suit up!"

Alegro flew across the room to wrap around a startled Felipe. Red magical trails swirled around Freddy, transforming him into Lobo. Jumping to his feet, Joshua activated his sentry gauntlets. Aiden and Aspen stood, transforming into the heroes in heels, Fire and Ice.

Shadow Guardian looked at Alex, still in his civilian garb. "I said suit up."

"I don't have my suit." Alex crossed his arms. "Why would I? This was supposed to be a celebration dinner, not a battle."

Lobo took Gato by the wrists. "Gato, I don't want to hurt you. Let Esmerelda go." Lobo let go to avoid a black paw from Gato's arm digging into him. He barely got out a, "What the Hell," when a huge black jaguar flew from Gato's arms, pinning Lobo to the ground with a snarling hiss.

"I'm never having dinner here again," Felipe lamented, letting Alegro pull him along with Juan Carlos to safety.

Diego scolded Alex, who remained seated, "You should always carry your suit with you!"

"Focus! Stop them!" Esmerelda shouted.

Fire lifted her hand to shoot a fireball, but only a tiny flame appeared on her fingertip. "Seriously?"

"What is going on here?" Boots asked, looking about, confused.

Keagan opened the tiny box to reveal a gold ring with a flat top that was emblazoned with the outline of a cat's paw in silver. "It's beautiful." Keagan slipped on the ring. He felt knowledge, memories, and power from previous champions surge into him. Picking up the baton, he stood. Holding it in front of him, Keagan proclaimed, "Boots is under my protection. An assault on him is an assault on me."

The two lionesses turned and roared to accentuate the proclamation. A double helix of pink mystical energy swirled from Keagan's ring over him, leaving pink fur armor in its wake, along with a long whipping tail, matching domino mask, and ears.

"Keagan. You're pink," Boots whispered loudly.

Keagan put down the arm holding his baton and looked at Boots. "I know. I like pink. It's my favorite color."

"Your fur is soft," Boots said, running his hand along Keagan's arm.

Slumping his shoulders, Keagan sighed. "You can pet me later. We're in the middle of a battle."

"You mean losing a battle. I hope that gaudy pink fur keeps you warm." Ice shot a blast of cold at Keagan.

Instinctively, he twirled the baton one-handed, sending the blast back at her. Joshua jumped in front of her, shields raised to absorb the ricocheting blast.

Fire tapped her chin thoughtfully. "I like it. Pink is in, and the ears are too cute!"

"Actually, I do too," Ice admitted. "I was trying to be a badass."

Lowering his shields, Joshua asked, "Am I the only one that wants to see him with whiskers?"

"I could draw them on him if you want," Boots offered innocently.

Diego threw his hands up in frustration. "Guys, this is not witty banter time with the enemy!"

"I don't know. The whiskers might be a bit much," Juan Carlos added.

With his pink tail whipping around, Keagan put his hand on his hip. Waving the baton with his other hand, he asked, "These are the people who foiled Doug Trainer and his Pup Patrol?"

"To be fair, it was me and the Lunarray wolves that defeated them," Lobo growled from underneath the panther. "Hey, Salvador, a little help here?"

Salvador crossed his arms over his chest. "You didn't want my help on patrol, so why would you want it now?" He huffed, "Suffer in your toxic masculinity."

"I am so confused about what's going on here," Boots commented, scratching his head.

Felipe sighed. "You learn to just roll with it."

Alex noticed Chitter and Fierce merrily playing on the coffee table. He reached behind him and tapped Salvador's thigh. He motioned over to the two playing. Alex reached over and interrupted the playing by scratching Fierce on the head. He purred happily.

Fierce let out a cheerful "Meow."

"We'll come back when you guys work through your relationship problems and get your acts together. How's next Tuesday for you?" Keagan suggested.

Struggling against Gato's grip, Esmerelda hissed, "You're not going anywhere!"

"Is that so?" Alex said to Fierce.

Fierce whipped his tail back and forth with a serious "Meow."

"Salvador, can you bring some order to this chaos?" Alex asked.

Shadow Guardian turned his attention to Alex and Salvador. "What are you two up to?"

"I've got this." Salvador closed his eyes then let out a harmony in B minor.

Purple magic flowed about the room, wrapping around everyone. Diego's suit deactivated. Fire and Ice were transformed back to Aiden and Aspen. Joshua's shields deactivated. The fierce felines were lifted and returned to Gato's arms. Gato released Esmerelda. Lobo became Freddy again. Magical circular binds surrounded the heroes, preventing them from using their powers.

Esmerelda struggled against her bonds. "What are you doing, Salvador?"

"Hey, guys!" Aaron yelled from the door. "Sorry we're late!"

Demona, Dion, Aaron, and Doctor Tyson appeared in the entryway.

Aiden brightened. "Hey, Tyson! Dinner is going to be a little bit delayed."

"Why does none of this surprise me?" Demona asked Dion. She pointed at Boots. "You!"

CHAPTER 7

D ION PUT HER HAND ON HER HEAD. "Do I need to ask?"

"It all started when Alex said he was my daddy," Diego began.

Dion held up her hand to stop him. "I don't want to hear about your daddy issues."

"He does seem to be fixated on the whole daddy thing," Aaron commented to Doctor Tyson. "Remind me to tell you about the first time I officially met him."

Taking his glasses off to clean them, Doctor Tyson said, "I read the report." Putting his glasses back on, he squinted at Keagan. "Is he wearing a pink cat suit?"

"I think he needs whiskers," Aiden chimed in.

Keagan rolled his eyes. "Again with the pink and whiskers. Can we go back to talking about

Diego Sanz's daddy issues or start talking about wolf boy's toxic masculinity?"

"Wolf boy!" Freddy shouted, offended.

Diego laughed. "That is totally your new nickname."

"Totally," Salvador agreed with a laugh.

Boots asked, "Can I have a nickname?"

"Your nickname is vanquished!" Esmerelda shouted, struggling against the magical bonds. "As soon as I get out of this... Salvador! Release me!"

Eyes flashing, one red and one white, Demona ordered, "Don't you dare."

"Oh, I wasn't." Salvador crossed his arms. "I know the consequences."

Dion kissed Demona's cheek. "Perhaps you should take this to neutral ground?"

"Unfortunately, yes." Demona swirled her wrists, creating a portal to In Between. "Kitty boy and... I'm sorry. I don't know your name."

"Meow," Fierce chimed in happily.

Demona sucked in her lips to keep from laughing. "Their names are what?"

"I am not being called Puss!" Keagan snapped.

Diego started laughing. "That is too funny!"

"Right?" Demona openly laughed.

Puzzled, Alex looked at Diego then at Keagan and Boots. His eyes grew wide with amusement, then he started laughing. "I'm sorry. I don't mean to laugh."

"What's so funny?" Juan Carlos asked.

"I don't know," Boots answered, confused. "Keagan, what's so funny about us being called Puss and Boots?"

The room erupted in laughter. Taking Boots' hand, Keagan grumbled angrily, "I don't know where this goes, but it's got to be better than here." Pulling Boots to the portal, he shouted, "Fierce! Are you coming?!"

"Meow," Fierce answered, jumping from the table to follow them.

Stepping through the portal, Keagan, Boots, and Fierce found themselves in the middle of In Between. Keagan positioned himself in front of Boots when he saw the muscular black man with dreads coming toward them. He nearly jumped when he felt a hand on his shoulder. Turning, he saw it was the woman who had created the portal.

CHAPTER 8

KISSING DION ON THE CHEEK, SHE said, "I'll call you later." To Esmerelda, she curtly said, "Remember the laws of In Between."

"Demona!" Esmerelda yelled angrily as Demona stepped through the portal. A moment later, the portal closed.

With the portal closed with Keagan, Boots, and Fierce safely on the other side, Salvador sang an F-sharp, breaking the binding rings around everyone.

"So are we having dinner first before heading over to In Between?" Freddy asked, stretching. Slack-jawed, everyone stared at him. "What? Wolf metabolism, remember?"

Angrily, Esmerelda said, "Grab a snack, wolf boy. We're heading over to In Between." She pointed at Salvador and Alex. "Give me a good reason for not banishing you two to a Hell dimension."

"You'll have to go through me," Diego warned, stepping in front of Alex.

Doing the same to Salvador, Freddy added, "Back off, Esmerelda."

"You would have hurt an innocent being," Salvador answered, moving Freddy aside. "He's not a demon."

Unconvinced, Esmerelda gentled her tone. "What are you talking about? You had to sense it." Salvador shook his head. "Gato? Freddy?" They shook their heads when she said their names.

"Fierce said Keagan was charged with protecting him," Alex added.

Confused, Esmerelda shook her head. "I sensed he was a demon." She looked at Gato. "And what was that with you and your cats protecting him? What were those magical items they gave him?"

"I don't know." Gato cautiously took her in his arms. "You know I would never hurt you, but the cats couldn't let you hurt Puss."

Diego raised a finger. "Are we seriously calling him that? It just doesn't seem right."

"I vote for what Demona called him. Kitty Boy." Doctor Tyson pushed his glasses back up his nose. "That is if I get a vote."

Rushing over to his boyfriend, Aiden said, "Of course you get a vote." Kissing Doctor Tyson on the cheek, he said, "I vote Kitty Boy too."

"If we're voting, yeah. I have to go with Kitty Boy," Aspen chimed in.

Shrugging, Joshua asked, "What's wrong with the Pink Puss?" He winced after he said the name. "Never mind. I heard it. I vote for Kitty Boy."

"So we're glossing over the fact that my personal assistant is some sort of ancient kitty champion?" Felipe asked, looking around. "We're all good with that?"

Patting his son on the shoulder, Juan Carlos said sympathetically, "Aiden and Aspen are elemental Drag Queens."

"I'm part Lunar Wolf," Freddy chimed in.

Raising his hand, Gato said, "I'm technically a mystical cat."

"New species of Siren," Salvador added.

"I'm dating a half angel, half demon," Dion added casually.

Joshua shrugged. "I'm in a poly relationship with a Drus and a former evil bear."

"Dating Diego," Alex added impishly.

Offended, Diego shot Alex an angry look. "Hey!

"Alex wins," Juan Carlos announced. Following the collective murmurs of agreement, he said to Felipe, "It's like a typical Monday for us."

Huffing, Diego crossed his arms. "Need I remind everyone that most of you work for me directly or indirectly?"

"I was teasing." Alex kissed Diego on the cheek.

Tugging on Aspen's pant leg, Chitter asked, "When can Fierce come back to play?"

"I don't know," Aspen said, picking up the robotic squirrel and snuggling them close.

Massaging her temples, Esmerelda groaned. "For once, can we stay on topic? New rule." She extended one hand. Blue and white sparks danced on her fingertips. "Go off topic and you get an electric shock. Understood?" She aimed her sparking hand at Salvador. "What do you mean he's an innocent and not a demon?"

"I didn't sense any demon in him, and Fierce said he's not a demon, not really," Salvador answered.

Chitter chirped, "Fierce said they were charged with protecting him at all costs."

"Fierce could speak to you?" Aspen asked, looking down at them.

Chitter twitched his whiskers. "Yeah. Duh, I know how to speak cat."

"We need answers, and we're only going to get them at In Between," Esmerelda proclaimed. "Let's go."

Reading her phone, Dion held up a hand. "Wait. Demona texted me. She says she'll open a portal to In Between in an hour or so after she's gotten everything sorted out and to, quote, 'Tell Esmerelda not to get her panties in a knot,' end quote."

"So it's okay to eat, then?" Freddy asked hopefully.

Rolling her eyes, Esmerelda answered, "Well, since we have the time and the food is ready."

CHAPTER 9

Sitting with boots in the strange bar, Keagan glared over at Demona talking to Fierce in some strange bubble. "She's been talking to Fierce for over thirty minutes." Keagan glanced at his wrist then realized his smart watch was covered by the strange magical fur armor. "I think."

"She said it was a privacy bubble." Boots reached out and took his hand. "Keagan, I'm scared. Why did that woman want to hurt me? Why are those two looking at me with anger in their eyes?"

Keagan interlaced his fingers with Boots. He didn't understand the fondness he had for the mysterious twunk or why Boots returned that same fondness. It felt right, like they were destined to find one another and that fate brought them together.

"Don't worry," Keagan reassured him. "I'll protect you." Turning his head, he hissed at Herc and Ryuu by the bar, "This is a bar, isn't it? How about some drinks?"

Ryuu's scales glittered under his skin. Moving behind the bar, he kept an eye on the two as he poured white liquid into two glasses. When he carried the glasses over, his scales noticeably rippled under his muscled body. Shooting daggers at Boots with his eyes, he carefully set the glasses down.

"Milk? A little speciesist," Keagan growled.

A bit of resentment seeped into Ryuu's normal flat tone. "I thought kittens liked milk."

"This kitten is lactose intolerant," Keagan hissed. His eyes caught the shimmer of Ryuu's scales. "What are you? Some magical iguana?"

Ryuu's nostrils flared with smoke and fire. "I'm a dragon." Ryuu snatched the glasses from the table. "Remember that, Champion."

"Am I lactose intolerant?" Boots asked when Ryuu left the table.

Keagan smiled warmly at Boots. "I don't know, but this isn't the time or place to find out."

"Two black cherry sodas." Herc sat two glasses with almost pitch black liquid in them. "A little advice, kid. Don't piss off the dragon."

Keagan stared defiantly at the black muscle god, then relented. "Tell him I'm sorry. He did bring me milk, though."

"I know." Herc cracked a smile.

Boots took a cautious sip from his glass. His eyes brightened with delight. Picking up the glass, he downed half of the soda in one gulp. Herc and Keagan looked at Boots with confusion when he started giggling.

"The bubbles tickle my nose," Boots said between giggles.

Smiling at Boots' amusement, Keagan said, "He's sort of new."

"I know." Herc shook his head in disbelief. "I'll get you two another round."

Boots finished his soda then smiled at Keagan with blackish-purple stained lips and teeth. "I like black cherry soda!"

"I'll get you some for the apartment." Keagan smiled. He liked that he got to see Boots experience these simple things for the first time. It was like he got to relive them vicariously through Boots.

Keagan took a sip of his soda. His eyes went wide with surprise at the rich, sweetly tart flavor. "That is so good!" he exclaimed.

"I'm glad you like it." Ryuu appeared, setting two more glasses down.

Keagan was momentarily entranced by the scales shimmering under his skin. Looking into Ryuu's stern eyes, he meekly said, "I'm sorry for calling you an iguana."

"Apology accepted." Ryuu's expression softened. "The milk was speciesist. I'm sorry."

Keagan smiled, feeling a little more at ease. "Apology accepted."

"Are you really a dragon?!" Boots burst out excitedly.

Ryuu looked at Boots with a mixed expression of hate and confusion. "What are you?"

"What do you mean?" Boots asked, shrinking back into the booth.

Sensing his discomfort, Keagan quickly answered, "He's a twunk." Seeing the confusion on Ryuu's face, he explained, "You know, a twink with muscles. A twunk." Seeing the bewilderment on Ryuu's face deepen, Keagan continued, "Okay, you see a twink is—"

"I know what a twink and a twunk are," Ryuu cut him off. He studied Keagan's face. "You don't know, do you?" They all turned their attention to the almost imperceptible sound of Demona's privacy bubble lowering. "I'll leave it to Demona to explain," Ryuu said, walking away.

Watching Demona stand from her booth in the corner and pick up an obviously annoyed Fierce, Keagan slipped out of his side of the booth and in beside Boots. Watching the confident and self-assured woman with her white hair cascading down her shoulders, Keagan knew he should fear and respect her.

When Demona reached the table, she sat Fierce down on it. The feisty kitten looked back at Demona and flicked his tail up as he stuck up his chin with a chuff. Fierce spun around, then sat down to stare at Demona with a mildly annoyed look upon his furry face.

"Champion, your guardian is a smart-ass." Demona returned Fierce's annoyed look.

Fierce let out an unamused "Meow."

"Language!" Keagan quickly reprimanded. To Demona, he said, "I'm sorry. He watches a lot of cable television."

Demona slipped into the empty side of the booth. "I've been called worse by far bigger cats."

"Meow," Fierce said with a chuff.

Demona's eyes flared, one red and one white. "How would you like to find out how many ways there are to skin a cat?"

"He wouldn't." Boots pulled Fierce down into his lap. He whispered to Fierce, "Behave."

Demona's eyes returned to normal. She watched Boots and Keagan, seeing how they unconsciously moved closer to each other as they fussed over the kitten in Boots' lap. "How long have you two been together?" Demona asked, curiously studying the two.

"We're not together," Keagan said, quickly stiffening in his seat.

Boots looked up with his bright smile. "He lured me in off the streets and took me back to his apartment. We slept together after I took a shower."

"I rescued him off the street," Keagan clarified, slightly flustered. "Then we actually slept in the same bed, as in sleep."

Demona shook her head in disbelief. "Not another pair of goofball lovers."

"We're not lovers," Keagan blurted.

Boots thought for a moment. "Fierce says I'm supposed to be your boy toy." He looked at Keagan. "I meant to ask you what that meant."

"Don't listen to that kitten." Demona chuckled, shaking her head. "At least about that stuff."

Boots looked down at Fierce quietly snickering in his lap, then back at Demona. "Does that mean Keagan is my boy toy?"

"No!" Keagan glared at Fierce. "You need to behave."

Demona sighed. "Let's get to the matter at hand." She motioned at Keagan. "You are obviously a Champion of Bastet, though you are the first pink one I've ever seen."

"I like pink." Keagan shrugged.

Demona shot a dirty look at Fierce. "Despite what your guardian says, I'm not calling you the Pink Puss."

"I like Kitty Boy," Boots piped up merrily.

Rolling his eyes with a hint of a smile, Keagan consented, "Since you like it, okay."

"They don't know, do they?" Demona asked Fierce.

Fierce let out a regretful "Meow."

"Know what?" Keagan looked to Boots, then Demona, and then to Fierce to whom he asked, "What do you mean not yet?"

Demona cleared her throat to get everyone's attention back. "You'll know when it's right. In the meantime, you," she motioned at Boots, "have caused quite a disturbance in the mystical community. A demon that is not a demon."

"He's not a demon," Keagan responded protectively, his body tensing and ready to fight.

Demona focused her attention on Keagan. "Chill, Kitty Boy. This is a neutral place. All beings are welcomed here without fear of harm." She raised an eyebrow and looked at Fierce. "Unless they make me mad." Fierce ducked down below the table. "Now, if you're done fluffing up your fur, can we continue?"

"I'm sorry. I'm protective of Boots," Keagan explained, relaxing.

Boots put an arm around Keagan. "I'm protective of him too."

"Of course you are; you're—" Demona stopped when she saw Fierce's head pop up from under the table. "Never mind. Back to what I was saying." She motioned to Boots again. "Within you is the potential to be a demon. That is why Esmerelda wanted to attack you."

Confused, Keagan looked at Boots then at Demona. "Aren't demons hideous, grotesque creatures with horns and tails?"

"I'm half demon." Demona's eyes flared in warning.

Keagan shrank back. "Sorry."

"Forgiven." Demona's eyes returned to normal. "Boots has something in him called a Rage Seed." She narrowed her eyes at Boots, peering through the veils of magic. "His is different somehow. Like he has the potential for great good or great evil in him."

Boots stood up straighter. "I like good."

"Yes." Demona's eyes moved between the two. "I see that and that your seed is growing in an unusual way."

Concerned, Keagan asked, "Is it dangerous?"

"No." Demona shook her head. "Not as long as he has you by his side."

Boots grinned brightly. "You mean I get to be with Keagan forever?"

"As long as Fate and Destiny permit it." Demona smiled.

Keagan had a momentary flash of a memory. "Fate and Destiny and a strange old woman. They were there, standing over me the night I got hit by that SUV."

"Old woman?" Demona asked. "Wearing a bright colorful dress, maybe a head scarf holding back her hair?"

Keagan shook his head. "I don't know. It was there and now it's gone."

"I see." Demona pulled out her phone and began texting Dion. "I think it's time we brought the others here." She paused then deleted the message before retyping it. "Maybe just a few of them."

Boots took Keagan's hand in his. Fear filled his voice. "That lady isn't going to try to hurt me again, is she?"

"No one is going to hurt you as long as I'm around," Keagan growled.

Demona set her phone down. "Again, a neutral place. Everyone is safe here."

"Unless they make you mad," Boots said with a smile.

Returning his smile, Demona said, "Unless they make me mad."

"Don't make her mad," Boots whispered to Fierce.

Fierce chuffed an annoyed "Meow."

CHAPTER 10

D IEGO AND ALEX FOLLOWED
Esmerelda, Gato, and Salvador through
the portal into In Between. Before them stood
Demona, with Herc and Ryuu flanking her.
Behind them stood Keagan in his pink cat suit,
holding Fierce, and Boots beside him. Before the
portal closed, Chitter and Alegro jumped through.

"We brought food." Diego held up the bags he
brought, trying to ease the palpable tension in the
room. "You know, since you missed the dinner
Alex and I made."

Silence came from the other side until Fierce
noticed Chitter and Alegro hiding behind Alex
and Diego. He let out an excited "Meow!"

"Yes, you can play with your squirrel friend and
his buddy." Keagan set the kitten on the ground

when he saw Chitter peeking from behind Diego's leg and waving.

Fierce let out a reprimanding "Meow."

"I'm sorry." Keagan put his hands up in supplication. "Their friend," he corrected himself. "You're right. I should know better than to assume pronouns."

Diego looked down at his feet where Keagan and Fierce were looking to see Chitter and Alegro. Gently scolding, he said, "What are you two doing here?"

"We wanted to play with Fierce." Chitter made their eyes big and black. "Please! Alegro didn't get to play with him." Alegro vibrated beside Chitter. "Right, and you didn't say we couldn't come."

Alex's phone rang. Answering it, he said, "Hey, Juan Carlos. Yes, they are here. Yes, they are okay. Alright, I'll tell them." Hanging up the phone, he addressed Chitter and Alegro. "You two are grounded."

"You're not really grounded," Diego told them with a wink. "Now go play with your friend." Watching Chitter and Alegro meet Fierce in the middle then rush away to play, Diego smiled. He held up the bags he was holding. "Peace offering? I brought food."

Alex took one of the bags and headed over to Herc. "There would have been more, but you know—Freddy."

"Yeah, I know." Taking the bags, Herc let out a boisterous laugh. "He's the reason we don't have bottomless wings night anymore."

Diego took Alex's lead and went over to Ryuu. "What do you guys say? Can we go back to being friends?"

"Is that...?" Ryuu sniffed the air, then took the bag from Diego and sniffed it. "It is!"

Diego smiled proudly. "Actually, they are my croquettes, but I used Juan Carlos's recipe." To Keagan and Boots, he said, "Sorry for, you know, inviting you over to dinner then threatening and attacking you. Our bad."

"It happens," Boots said merrily. To Keagan, he asked, "Does it?"

Keagan growled. "No. It doesn't." He pointed his baton at Esmerelda. "Is she going to try and hurt Boots again?" Everyone looked at a disapproving Esmerelda. "I can feel her gathering her magic."

"Esmerelda!" Demona's eyes glowed. "You know the rules of In Between. Don't make me bind you."

Gato put a hand on her shoulder. "The rules apply to him as well. We are safe here."

"Fine." Esmerelda released the magic she was gathering. "I still say he is a demon."

The light faded from Demona's eyes. "He is and he isn't. This calls for a parley of sorts." Demona raised both hands and snapped her fingers. A rectangular table and chairs rose from the floor. "Diego, Alex, and Salvador will sit in those three seats." She pointed to one long side. "Herc, Ryuu, and I will take these three." The three took the seats opposite of where she directed the others. "I assume the rest of you know where you belong."

"I'm not sure where I belong," Boots said, looking around.

Keagan took him by the hand and sat him at the table so Ryuu was to his left. "You belong beside me." Keagan sat beside him. "Don't worry. I'll protect you."

"We'll see about that, Kitty Boy." Esmerelda sat in the chair opposite Boots, but as soon as she did, her chair and the empty one for Gato swapped places so she sat across from Keagan and Salvador was to her left.

Keagan rolled his eyes. "I guess that name is sticking."

"Meow!" Fierce cried out teasingly, amusing Chitter and Alegro.

Keagan blanched. "No! I will not be called that!"

"That kitten has one foul mouth," Gato said, shaking his head as he took the seat beside Esmerelda.

Exasperated, Keagan agreed. "I came home today to find he taught Boots several new inappropriate words and phrases."

"Yeah, he told me that the appropriate way to say hello to someone was what's up—" Boots was cut off by Keagan's hand covering his mouth.

Removing his hand, Keagan explained, "It's also not appropriate to tell people what inappropriate words and phrases you know."

"Okay, I got to ask," Diego spoke up. "The pink fur. Is it some sort of metallic armor? How does it work?"

Keagan held out his arms. "It's magical skin armor. It sort of is my skin and not."

"He's also really adorable in it," Boots added, grinning from ear to ear.

Diego raised an eyebrow. "Why do you have ears, though?"

"Duh, I'm a cat." Keagan pointed at his ears, causing everyone to chuckle.

Regaining his composure, Salvador spoke up. "Can we get to the matter at hand? I need to get back to Wolf Boy." Salvador winked at Keagan. "I am calling him that for now on, so you know."

"Yes," Esmerelda said tersely, staring Keagan in the eyes, "let's get down to business. Why did this champion defend a demon?"

Keagan snarled, "He is not a demon."

"Didn't Demona say I was and I wasn't?" Boots looked at Demona. "I still don't get that."

Alex looked at Boots, then Demona, then to Esmerelda. "So Esmeralda was right?"

"And wrong?" Gato added.

Esmerelda glared at Demona. "You're being awfully quiet. Do you want to enlighten us?"

"Certainly." Demona grinned wickedly. She motioned to Keagan. "Kitty Boy is a Champion of Bastet, I believe. We'll come back to him in a minute." She motioned to Boots. "Boots, as he likes to be called, has potential. He has an unusual Rage Seed in him."

Esmerelda glared at Boots. "Then we stifle that potential and end him now."

"Esmerelda, you know that's not how it works," Salvador jumped in. "You see the potential for great evil in him. I see the potential for great good in him."

Gato took Esmerelda's hand in his. "You have been looking for evil everywhere; it could be skewing your magical perception of Boots. A guardian and a champion wouldn't be tasked to protect a demon."

"And who tasked him?" Esmerelda flung her hand at Keagan. "Why in the world would anyone in their right mind make him a champion?"

Demona laughed. "Oh, you're going to love that answer." She leaned forward and spoke the name with amusement. "Madame Zelda."

"What?" Esmerelda's face fell. "You're lying."

Demona shook her head. "The Queen of the Gitanas is manipulating things somehow. Why Destiny and Fate are allowing her to do so, I don't know, but she is." She pointed at Gato. "He has a human form." She pointed at Salvador. "She raised him and guided him to me." She pointed at Esmerelda. "She returned your magical charms."

"She must have placed Kitty Boy's magical charms in my tattoos." Gato rubbed his arms. "How could she know to do that?"

"There were whispers in Spain that she may have been the one that awakened the knight errant," Esmerelda added. "By any chance, have you heard anything about a rogue knight and his magician?"

Demona looked to Herc then Ryuu, who shook their heads no. "I haven't. What names should we be listening for?"

"Don't laugh, but his name is Don. Don Quixote. His magician's name is Sancho Panza," Esmerelda answered. "Don comes from a wealthy family, and when he was awakened, he found Sancho and then the two disappeared."

Alex turned to Diego beside him. "Those guys at the resort."

"They were from Spain, and the tall one kept calling you Carmelo," Diego finished the thought.

Esmerelda glared at them. "What are you two talking about?"

"The stocky one, didn't he say he was a magician?" Alex continued, ignoring Esmeralda.

Diego snapped his fingers. "He did, and the tall one said he was a knight of the Spanish Court trying to right the wrongs of the world?"

"We just thought they were eccentric." Alex's eyes grew wide.

Annoyed, Keagan spoke up. "Excuse me!" Diego and Alex looked at him. "I know it's rude to make something about yourself, but you know this sort of is about me and Boots. Can we table your fancy resort talk until after?"

"He got them to be quiet. We're definitely keeping him." Demona smiled. "Back to Madam Zelda." She shot a dirty look over at Fierce rolling on the floor with Alegro and Chitter. "Kitty Boy's guardian was no help, but I was able to piece together from Keagan that it is a definite possibility Madam Zelda turned him into a champion."

Keagan reached over and took Boots' hand. "Fierce said I was tasked with protecting Boots, but he didn't say from whom."

"I think he has a magical block," Demona explained. "He knows it but is forbidden to tell us much more than he gives us." She shook her head. "The attitude is all him."

Keagan looked at Boots. "Fierce said I had to protect him. I don't know why, but I felt it deep inside me when I saw Boots." He took Boots' hand. "It feels like we were fated to meet, destined to be in one another's lives."

"You are what tips the scale," Ryuu said. "Good or evil, you are the one that will be the catalyst for Boots being one or the other."

As he squeezed Keagan's hand, Boots' voice trembled. "I don't want to be evil and mean like the guards and people in white coats." Eyes watering with fear, he pleaded, "Keagan, don't let me become evil."

Alegro, Fierce, and Chitter came bounding onto the table in front of Boots. Alegro wrapped himself around the young man while Fierce jumped into his lap and Chitter gave him a hug.

"Don't worry, Boots," Chitter chirped. "We'll protect you. You're family now."

Taking Keagan's other hand, Diego said, "Chitter is right. You're family now. Both of you."

He then addressed the table. "I don't know or even want to pretend to know what forces are bringing us together. It's obvious they have a purpose, and we'll do better protecting each other than fighting one another."

"Agreed." Esmerelda waved her hand around flippantly. "I won't vanquish him until he becomes a full-fledged demon."

Salvador warned, "Esmerelda, you know even then you can't just vanquish him. He has to do something to deserve vanquishing."

"Demons always do something to make them deserve vanquishing." Esmerelda leaned back in the chair. "Okay, what do we do with him?"

Keagan snarled, "He has a name. It's Boots, and he stays with me."

"Agreed," Demona proclaimed. "Keagan is key in Boots' future. We do need to keep them both close."

Salvador volunteered, "They are moving into Alex's old apartment. Freddy and I are downstairs. Esmerelda is just a few blocks away."

"We can have Shadow Drones monitor the outside," Alex added. "We can all take shifts watching the outside at night."

Diego looked at Keagan and Boots, then to the rest of the table. "Have we asked what they want? It is their lives, after all."

"We were going to take the apartment anyway." Keagan looked at Boots and saw the fear in his face. "I want to make sure Boots is safe. Fierce will be with him when I'm not. Knowing you all are there to help protect him will put me a little more at ease." Keagan shook his head. "I can't help but feel something bad is on its way."

Herc cleared his throat. "That's why he has caused such a disturbance in the mystical community."

"What do you mean?" Gato motioned to him and Esmerelda. "We just got back from Spain. What's going on?"

Demona put her hands together in front of her. "That is the next thing we have to discuss. It's also the reason why we have to protect Boots." Her eyes darted around the table. "Boots escaped from the Demon Twink. Ryuu has gotten confirmed reports from various mystical creatures that are spying him."

"That means he'll be coming for Boots." Diego turned to Alex. "You need to be ready. We need to step up your training."

Alex groaned. "I can't believe I wanted to be your sidekick once."

"You all need to be ready," Demona continued. "Who knows what he'll send after you this time to get Boots back?"

86

Boots hugged Chitter close. "You don't think he'll send those mean three bears after me, do you?"

"There's only two bears now," Diego corrected. "Teddy is now in the woods with Jack. He's no longer part of their crew."

Boots shook his head. "No. There are three bears. Sometimes they would be in the lab at the same time as me." Boots shivered. "They would growl and say mean things to me until they were done running those tests on us." Boots smiled. "I remember Teddy. Well, seeing him. He was in the cell across from me. He used to say nice things to me after..."

"After they beat him," Keagan finished. "He's been through a lot in his short life."

Curious, Alex asked, "Boots, how old are you?"

Boots looked to Keagan, who answered for him. "He's about three weeks old. He was grown in a lab."

"Ryuu," Demona looked at him, "we need information."

Standing up, he said, "On it."

"We'll do what we can to help you, but do not expect much help from the mystical community. None want to draw the attention of the Demon Twink." Demona stood. "There is a battle coming. You need to prepare. We need to prepare." She hugged herself. "I fear the fallout from this is bigger than we can imagine."

CHAPTER 11

G AYMER SLAMMED HIS FIST DOWN on the table, shaking the parts and tools on it. *This is impossible!* He fought the urge to swipe the table clear of everything. Leaning back in the chair, he closed his eyes. *I have to do this for Uncle Doug.*

Gaymer felt strong hands massaging his shoulders. "That feels great," he said without thinking. His eyes flew open, and he bolted out of the chair. He turned to see Finn standing there. "What do you think you're doing?!"

"Making sure you're comfortable, of course." Finn grinned mischievously. "A happy worker is a productive worker."

Gaymer ground his teeth in anger. "I'm not your worker. I'm your prisoner."

"Worker, prisoner. Does it really matter what we call you?" Finn waved his hand in the air dismissively. "It really doesn't matter, doesn't it?"

Gaymer wanted to throttle him but knew better. Hostility obvious, he asked, "What do you want?"

"I know what it is like being locked up in a room with nothing but your thoughts to keep you company," Finn answered, a touch of sympathy in his voice. "I thought you'd like to go for a stroll in the corridors. No agenda. Just a casual stroll. You don't have to talk if you don't want to."

Gaymer held up his wrist with the magical bracelet. "Taking your pet out on a leash? Is that what you want to do?" Gaymer sneered. "No, thank you."

"What else do you have to do?" Finn asked with a slight hint of pleading in his voice. "Look, you're stressed and I'm bored. A walk will do us both good."

Refusing to let his guard down, Gaymer asked, "How am I supposed to get out that door?"

"Take my hand and I'll show you." With an uncharacteristically warm smile, Finn extended his hand.

Cautiously, Gaymer took it. In a puff of smoke, they were outside. The foul smell of brimstone burned Gaymer's nose and caused his eyes to water. The acrid taste in his mouth caused him to cough.

"Here." Finn pressed a water bottle to his lips. Gaymer drank greedily, trying to douse the fire in his throat. "I'm sorry. I should have remembered to put a protective bubble around you." Finn helped him to the ground. "Dante normally transports people, not me."

Wiping his mouth with the back of his hand, Gaymer looked at Finn with red stinging eyes. "Dante seems to do a lot. What are you to him?"

"I'm his servant, his protector, and his husband." A wet cloth appeared in Finn's hand. He pressed it to Gaymer's eyes. "He's more my protector than I am his. He bound me to him when he didn't have to. Sure, he did it by trickery, but he didn't have to. He could have let the Gitana banish me back to a Hell dimension, but because of our mate bond, I was brought back to him."

Gaymer finished the last of the water with a dry cough. "He treats you like a slave from what I saw."

"What you saw is what we wanted you and everyone to see." Finn pulled the cloth away. "Better?" Gaymer nodded. Taking him by the hand, Finn lifted them both to their feet. "When we are alone, he is surprisingly gentle and caring with me."

Brushing the grass from his pants, Gaymer pointed out, "He said you could be replaced."

"That's what you were meant to hear." Finn laughed. He started walking. "Come. We'll talk while we walk." Finn waited until Gaymer was beside him. "Dante and I put on a show for everyone. Love is seen as a weakness by most in the demon world. I will not have him perceived as weak."

Gaymer pondered for a moment the likelihood of his being able to run away and escape but remembered his deal with Finn. His uncle and Brutus depended on his cooperation. "What about you? Why do you have to be weak for him to be strong?"

"I am not weak. Yes, we give that illusion that I am, but I am far from weak." Finn laughed. "At first, Dante only funneled what power I needed into me to serve him. Now, he gorges me with power. The only reason I wasn't able to fend off the Drus was because I made Dante hoard his power for when he was in Morgan City."

Gaymer kicked at the ground. "It sounds like you love him."

"I would burn this world for him," Finn answered. "And I have no doubt he would do the same for me."

Gaymer hugged himself. Awkwardly, he asked, "How do you know if you love someone?"

"You just do." Finn stopped and put a hand on Gaymer's shoulder. "I could get in trouble for this, but if you'd like, I can get a message to Ice that you are still alive."

Gaymer's heart leapt for joy, but he quickly grew suspicious. "Why would you do that for me?"

"Consider it a," Finn thought for a moment for the right word, "favor."

Gaymer scoffed in derision. "And what favor would I need to do for you in return?"

"Nothing. I only ask that this small act of kindness inspires you to do the same in return." Finn started to walk again. "I grow weary of this partnership Dante has gotten himself in. I do not trust they have our best interest at heart or share our same goals."

Gaymer mulled the words over. *That's the chink in the armor.* To Finn, he said, "Okay. What are your goals?"

"Oh, you know. What every demon twink wants," Finn answered cryptically. "Too bad I have to take you back soon. It's nice to be outside in the real world, don't you think?"

Gaymer ignored the question, choosing to ask his own. "When will you send Ice the message?"

"I already did," Finn answered with a smug smile.

"Okay, read it back to me." Dante stopped when he heard nothing. He looked at Death Drop sitting at a desk, busily scribbling on a piece of paper with her tongue stuck out the side of her closed mouth. Annoyed, Dante asked out loud, "Why couldn't Lip-Sync have a normal apprentice?"

Death Drop looked up and scowled at Dante.

"Don't look at me like that." Dante snatched the paper from the desk. "You have your uses in the field, but that's about it."

Dante looked at the paper, then at Death Drop. Certain he was mistaken in what he saw on the paper, he looked at the paper again. Lowering it, he tried to contain his anger before addressing Death Drop.

"I have been talking for the better part of an hour. Plans, details, contingency plans, escape plans, and more." The room shook with Dante's contained anger. "The only thing you had to do was write it down. Actually, you could have typed it or even recorded it, but instead, you drew this!"

Dante flung his arm out, showing Death Drop the childlike drawing she was working on. "You drew a chicken!" Dante's voice boomed with anger. Cracks zigzagged down the walls and across the ceiling. "A chicken! It's not even a good drawing either!"

Death Drop stuck out her lower lip, and tears began to stream out of her eyes. She then waved a hand over her face, changing it. Her eyes glowed red with anger. She bared her razor-sharp teeth in a silent hiss. Putting her hands on the desk, she stood up, knocking her chair to the ground.

"You dare threaten me." Dante looked at her unimpressed. He waved his hand, sending her crashing into the far wall. He held her pinned there. "Remember your place." Dante's voice thundered in the room. He held up the paper with the other. It slowly burned away starting at the bottom. "If I have to remind you again, it will not go well for you."

Dante dropped his hand, allowing Death Drop to fall to the ground. "I need Lip-Sync here." He began pacing again, turning his back on Death Drop. "She has more finesse." Dante twirled his wrist, sending a stalking Death Drop spiraling into a wall. "Let that serve as your final warning."

Death Drop fell upon the floor face down.

"Be advised that if this mission is not a success before Lip-Sync's return, it will not look good for you." Dante turned to see Death Drop laying sprawled out on the ground, Xs over eyes and mouth agape with her tongue out off to the side. He snarled, "If you do not get out of my sight this very instant, I will drain you of all your power and turn you into a fly so I can watch you experience the agony of a mortal death over and over again!"

With a plume of purple smoke, Death Drop disappeared.

"Good help is so hard to summon." Dante released a disillusioned sigh. He found himself standing by the table where Finn's bottle sat. He ran his hand over the smooth curves. *Soon, my dear Finn, we will have the army we need and be done with this cursed alliance and these bumbling fools.*

Doctor Gingerman sat in his chair with the white dog curled up on a large fluffy red bed beside him. Speaking aloud, he said, "It won't be long until all the pieces will be in place. We'll remake the world in our own image." The dog looked up at him with a growl. "Patience, my dear."

A pounding knock interrupted his thoughts. *Those damn bears are here. I'll be glad when they have outlived their usefulness.* He reached down and scratched the top of the dog's head. "Come," he bellowed.

The door opened to reveal the gruff Papa Bear with his wild reddish hair and beard. His body was bulkier than before with the adjusted mix devised from Teddy's blood. It had eased his temperament, allowing him to focus on combat skills, and it gave their new accidental bear a firm hold over them.

Stepping in, Papa snarled, "You wanted to see us?"

"Where are the other two?" Doctor Gingerman snapped. He hated dealing with them one-on-one.

A slender muscular man with wild eyes and a manic expression on his face came through the door. "Honey Bear is here!" he announced excitedly, rubbing his hands together. "Are we going to go out and cause some havoc?"

"Sit." Doctor Gingerman motioned to the couch. "I don't feel like repeating myself. Where is the other one?"

Gliding into the room was a Bear Drag Queen in a form-fitting pink and purple bodysuit, wearing a purple beehive wig as well as a matching color beard with white clown makeup and elaborate purple makeup. Eloquently, she spoke in a soft, deep voice. "Mama Bear has arrived." She took a seat beside Honey Bear. "What can we do for you?"

"We'll be going to Morgan City in the morning," Doctor Gingerman addressed only Mama Bear. "Our mission is to capture Experiment B12," he emphasized the next word, "*alive*."

Papa Bear made a show of cracking his knuckles. "What if he has an unfortunate accident?"

"Mama." Doctor Gingerman motioned to her. Sighing, she touched her bracelet. Papa Bear bolted up, then fell to the ground, twitching and screaming in pain. When he was satisfied, Doctor Gingerman motioned for Mama Bear to stop. "Let's just say," he addressed the still spasming Papa Bear, "it's in your best interest to ensure he comes back to us alive and intact."

Honey Bear grumbled, "It's not like we'd be able to enjoy the sounds of his screams anyway."

"What did I tell you about saying such things?" Mama Bear cuffed his head.

Honey Bear rubbed the back of his head. "Keep those thoughts in my head unless we're torturing someone or in battle."

"That's my sweet Honey Bear." Mama Bear patted him on the leg, causing Honey Bear to beam. "We'll be ready. When do we leave?"

Doctor Gingerman smiled proudly. Losing the man that became Mama had been a blow to his research, but she was more valuable as Mama in controlling the other two bears. "In the morning.

You'll each get a glamor charm from Dante. You'll be posing as my personal guard."

"Personal guard?" Papa Bear asked, picking himself up off the ground. "Why would you need a personal guard?"

Doctor Gingerman leaned back in the chair. "From your old buddy, Shadow Guardian." Papa Bear and Honey Bear growled. "Oh, and he has friends now."

CHAPTER 12

THE PORTAL BRINGING EVERYONE back from In Between had barely closed when a loud shrilling alarm from Aspen's phone went off. It was the exact same moment Chitter stood up on their hind legs, ears twitching and black eyes staring out into space. While everyone looked at Aspen for explanation, he looked to Chitter for confirmation as he silenced the alarm.

Chitter's eyes blinked. They gave Aspen a nod before letting out a bark to Alegro and Fierce. A moment later, the stairs leading down to Shadow Command opened up, and the three went bounding down with Aspen right behind them.

"What is going on?" Diego asked, looking to everyone for answers.

Realization struck Aiden. As he jumped up, his hair ignited. "Gaymer!" He rushed down the stairs, pulling Doctor Tyson's along with him.

"Who's Gaymer?" Boots asked, confused, watching everyone rush down the stairs.

Keagan shrugged. "I don't know, but Fierce is down there." He took Boots' hand. "Come on."

Downstairs, everyone was standing around watching Alegro busily whipping about his tendrils on the main console while Chitter sat in the chair analyzing the data that flashed across the screen rapidly. Fierce sat on the chair beside them, curiously watching the screen.

"They'll find him," Aiden said, putting his arm around his brother.

Aspen looked at his brother. Smiling at him, he said, "Your hair."

"I know." Aiden winked at him.

The screen slowed and turned into a map with a red dot on it. The screen changed to a real time satellite image of a facility in the woods. Boots gasped in fear. "I know that place." He grabbed onto Keagan. "Don't take me back there. Please, don't take me back there."

"I won't," Keagan reassured Boots, putting his arms around him. He gave the group a warning look. "I won't let anyone take you back there."

Fierce let out a curious "Meow."

"Yes, I see the strange magical auras too." Esmerelda stepped closer to the screen. "The building is interdimensional."

Juan Carlos came up alongside her. "What does that mean?"

"Your tracker shouldn't have been able to transmit," Esmerelda said bluntly. "Someone wanted it to be found. It could be a trap."

The air grew cold when Aspen spoke. "I don't care. I'm going to rescue Gaymer."

"Hold up, Aspen," Joshua said. "You and Aiden were barely able to hold your own against the Demon Twink. What do you think you can do alone?"

Esmerelda tapped a finger to her chin. "Yes, there is that too. I vanquished the Demon Twink," she turned to face the trio of new heroes, "but you three faced him, you said."

"Doug Trainer also said he was dealing with the Demon Twink," Aspen added. "Could there be more than one?"

Juan Carlos stepped forward. "Wait, Finn Andrews got married shortly after his father's passing and before you did your magical thing. He now runs the company. Could he be the Demon Twink in question?"

"We need answers," Diego spoke up. "We need to scout out that facility and get more information on the Demon Twink."

Alex added, "Not to mention find Doctor Gingerman. It was his device that Doug Trainer was using to control the Pups."

"Gato, I know we just got home." Esmerelda gave him a sympathetic look.

He nodded. "I'm with you."

"So am I." Freddy growled. "My wolf senses will be useful."

Salvador hugged his man. "I'm with you."

"Juan Carlos and I will reach out to the mystical community," Aaron suggested. "We've made quite a few connections that could help."

Chitter chirped, "Alegro and I will run the command center and keep everyone connected."

"The rest of us will keep protecting the city." Diego turned to Alex. "I hope you're up to it."

Alex grimaced. "I guess I had better."

"What about those two?" Esmerelda asked, pointing at Keagan holding Boots. "We can't ignore the fact that the Demon Twink wants Boots."

Keagan tightened his grip on Boots. "We'll do just fine on our own."

"You can't come to work in that pink fur," Felipe pointed out. "It might be a little distracting."

Fierce let out an unenthusiastic "Meow."

"I can tap the ring and the fur will go away?" Keagan glared at Fierce. "Why didn't you tell me that before?"

Fierce yawned, then answered, "Meow."

"Because Boots likes the fur is not a good enough reason." Keagan tapped his ring. Pink swirls of magic surrounded him and Boots, rescinding his fur, tail, and ears.

Boots pulled back to look at Keagan. "I liked the fur, but I like you like this too."

"We should get back home. It's getting late," Keagan said, trying to deflect the compliment.

Alex looked at Diego. Smiling when he saw the slight head nod, he addressed their guests. "Why don't you two stay here tonight, and tomorrow, Joshua can help you move into your new apartment? We can see what clothes we have that'll fit Boots better."

"I like wearing Keagan's clothes." Boots twisted around to address Alex, and the movement was accompanied by the sound of ripping fabric. "Uh oh."

Keagan groaned. "I'm not going to have any shirts left."

"It wasn't my shirt that tore," Boots whispered shyly in Keagan's ear. "If I turn around, they'll see my down there parts that make you blush. Is that okay?"

Keagan shot a snickering Fierce a dirty look. "Can I get a towel or something for Boots to cover up?"

"We can do better than that." Alex went to one of the wall panels. Pressing it revealed a small compartment. He took a Shadow Disc out. "This is a blank Shadow Disc." He tossed it to Keagan. "Put that on his chest, and it'll cover all of his," Alex smiled, "parts that make you blush."

Catching the disc, Keagan rolled his eyes at Alex. "How is this going to cover him?" He put the disc on Boots' chest, and the microbots spread out over his chest. "Hey! What's happening?!"

"They tickle." Boots laughed, spreading his arms and turning around in a circle once he was covered.

Alex picked up the programming remote. "Relax. Most of us wear similar suits."

"No." Aiden snatched the remote from Alex. "No more black!" He started typing in the remote. "We need a little more color on this team." The microbots on Boots started to change shape, causing Boots to giggle. "Plus, he needs to match Kitty Boy."

"My name isn't Kitty Boy," Keagan snapped. "It's Keagan."

Aiden waved his hand about dismissively. "I know. I'm talking about your alter ego." The microbots across Boots' chest changed into a square-cut, body-hugging athletic shirt while the bottom turned into loose fitting pants. "Now for some color." The straps turned pink and circled under Boots' arms and down his sides. The rest turned to an apple green. The pants turned into dark blue denim with a pink belt. "Better, and it matches his skin tone."

"I like it!" Boots turned about. "Keagan! Fierce! What do you think?!"

Fierce let out an approving "Meow."

"Well, it does fit you better," Keagan said, admiring him.

Aiden smiled wickedly. "Wait until you see his hero garb!" He typed into the remote, causing the microbots to change form again. The athletic shirt broke into crisscrossing pink stripes with apple green borders that barely covered his lean cut chest. The pants shrank into form-fitting shorts that stopped mid-thigh, with one side pink and the other apple green. "Oh, wait. A mask." Microbots traveled up Boots' face, making a pointed domino mask that started apple green in the center then slowly changed to pink to the edges. "Perfect."

"Nice," Keagan gulped, "but who said he's going to be a hero?"

Fierce let out an annoyed "Meow."

"He's right. You two were brought to us for a reason." Esmerelda stared intensely at Boots and Keagan. "How did I miss it?" Everyone looked at her. "Gato. Salvador. Freddy. Do you see it?"

Freddy put a hand over his heart. "I do now."

"I can't believe we missed it," Salvador said with a smile, putting an arm around Freddy.

Gato came up behind Esmerelda and put his arms around her. Kissing her on the cheek, he said, "Aren't you glad you didn't vanquish him?"

"What are we missing?" Diego asked in confusion.

Fierce let out a warning "Meow."

"Nothing we can share," Esmerelda said lovingly, putting her hands on top of Gatos. "Just know that we have to protect them at all costs."

Annoyed, Keagan growled, "Will someone tell me what you guys are talking about? Ryuu and Demona said the same thing."

"Meow," Fierce scolded.

Boots came up beside Keagan and put an arm around his waist. "Fierce is right. We'll know when we're supposed to know."

"Okay, Alex and I need to get ready for patrol tonight," Diego jumped in. "Joshua, why don't you take Keagan and Boots back to their place and get what they need for the night?"

Alex added, "Esmerelda, you should talk to Aspen and Aiden about their encounter with Madam Zelda." Alex snapped his fingers. "That reminds me. I think Diego and I ran into the guys you were looking for while we were on vacation."

"Don Quixote and Sancho Panza?" Esmerelda asked with wide eyes.

Alex blushed. "He called me his sweet Caramelo."

"He called me Alex's future ex-boyfriend," Diego spat bitterly.

Juan Carlos covered his mouth to hide his smile. "Diego, are you jealous?"

"He has no reason to be." Going to Diego, Alex hugged him. "I'd never leave Diego. Have you seen his butt?"

CHAPTER 13

"YOU'RE OKAY WITH ME SHARING a bed with you, right?" Boots asked, stepping out of the bathroom and into the bedroom. He was shirtless, wearing a pair of borrowed sleep pants from Alex that hung low on his hips. He fidgeted, waiting for Keagan's answer.

Keagan pulled the covers aside and patted the spot next to him. "I want you in my bed." Keagan felt a strange tingle in his chest from the words. He pulled the sheets up over Boots after he slipped in. *Why am I so drawn to him?* Boots snuggled against him. "A lot has happened. How are you doing with everything? We can hold off on the move if we need to."

Boots slipped a hand under Keagan's shirt and started rubbing his belly. Keagan involuntarily let out a purring sound. "I'm okay as long as I have you and Fierce." Boots laughed. "I like the way you purr."

Keagan grabbed Boots' hand through the sheet. "Stop that," he giggled. He let go of Boots' hand. "In five minutes. That feels really nice for some reason."

"Keagan, I know you're supposed to protect me, but I feel like I should protect you too." Boots ran his hand in circles over Keagan's belly. "Is that normal?"

Keagan chuckled. "I don't know what is normal anymore." He put an arm around Boots. "It's not normal, but we're not really normal. That's okay. Being different is okay. It makes us unique."

"Joshua said he would teach me how to defend myself." Boots lightly scratched Keagan's belly. "I like him. He's really nice. They all are, now that they aren't trying to hurt us."

Keagan stroked Boots' back. "It's strange how we're all connected, and they keep looking at us saying they see something that they can't tell us."

"Fierce knows too, but he won't or can't tell us. I guess we'll find out when we're supposed to, like they say." Boots shifted them so he was spooning Keagan. "We should get some sleep."

Keagan snuggled back against him. Yawning, he said, "I hope Fierce is behaving himself."

"Meow," Fierce instructed Alegro. They tapped at the console, bringing up a satellite map of Morgan City. Fierce studied the screen then let out another "Meow. Meow." A red line crossed the screen. Fierce's tail whipped back and forth. "Meow. Meow." Alegro made another red line across the screen that crossed the first.

Chitter stood up on their hind legs, studying the screen.

"Meow." Fierce cocked his head at the screen before letting out a second "Meow." A third red line drew across the screen, crossing the first at the same point the second did. "Meow," he instructed. Alegro zoomed in on the map. "Meow. Meow. Meow. Meow. Meow meow." Red lines appeared all over the screen, all intersecting at the same point as the first three.

Chitter cocked their head to the left then right. After they interfaced with the console remotely, seven blue circles appeared along the lines.

"Meow!" Fierce cried out, getting up on all fours.

"Um, should we be worried about what they are doing?" Aspen asked Aiden.

Aiden flipped the page of the book he was reading. "Naw." He glanced up to look at them. "What are they doing? What is that?"

"Chitter, what are you guys doing?" Aspen asked, walking over the console.

Chitter's whiskers twitched. "Fierce is showing us the ley lines of the city."

"Ley lines?" Aiden closed his book and joined his brother at the console.

Chitter turned to face them. "Ley lines are mystical lines of power that run over the planet. Where lines intersect are mystical power points."

"What are the blue circles?" Aiden asked, studying the screen.

Chitter looked at Fierce, who let out an affirmative "Meow."

"Keagan's apartment. In Between. Alex's old apartment. Esmerelda's brownstone. Your old apartment. DJC Tower and the DJC corporate headquarters," Chitter answered. "They all are along major ley lines that converge and eventually meet at the DJC Tower."

Aspen looked at Aiden who shrugged. "What does that mean?" he asked Chitter.

"Meow," Fierce answered gruffly.

Aspen rolled his eyes. "I'm sorry. It takes some time to get used to talking to a kitten."

"Yeah, and watch your language," Aiden chided. "We don't want Chitter and Alegro to have your litterbox mouth."

Chitter patted Fierce on the back. "It's okay. Our programming doesn't allow us to use such language."

"Meow," Fierce said merrily, then explained with, "Meow."

Aspen crossed his arms. "You don't know. You just feel more powerful here and wanted to know why?" He knelt down and looked Fierce in the eyes. "I'm not buying it, fur ball."

"He really doesn't know," Chitter interjected. "I was the one that pointed out the places of significance to us."

Fierce chuffed, "Meow."

"Send all this stuff to Esmerelda," Aspen ordered. Standing, he eyed Fierce suspiciously. "She might have some insight on it."

Aiden knelt to address Fierce. "It's getting late. Do you want me to take you to Keagan and Boots' room?"

"Meow," Fierce said gleefully.

Chitter laughed.

Alegro vibrated with amusement.

Aiden covered his mouth to hide his amusement.

"No, I don't think Keagan is," Aspen did his best to keep a straight face, "knocking Boots." He smiled. "Yet."

Resting his head on Finn's chest, Dante traced his fingertips along Finn's body. Bold in their private sanctuary, Finn confessed, "I don't trust Doctor Gingerman or the Head of the Board."

"Nor do I," Dante admitted. "That experiment they created felt off. Blasphemous. There's something they aren't telling us."

Finn covered Dante's hand with his, then interlaced their fingers. "They underestimate you."

"They underestimate us, my sinful delight," Dante corrected. "By keeping their eyes on me, they do not see what you do." Dante's eyes glowed red. "That will be their downfall, and soon, all of the Hell dimensions will tremble with fear at the mere mention of the Demon Twinks."

Finn rolled over on top of Dante. "Your ambition. Your drive. It's such a turn on." Magical sparks crackled when they kissed. "I can't believe you chose me to be yours."

"Believe it." Dante cradled Finn's face with his hand. "Your drive, ingenuity, and desire for power are a fire that drew me in." Magical sparks snapped and popped with their kiss. "The truth is you trapped me, and our bond grows stronger every day."

Finn's eyes glowed red with desire. "Allow me the privilege to show my gratitude for all you have done for me."

"After," Dante growled, rolling them over, "I show you my gratitude"

Doug Trainer stirred in his hospital bed. From the dim lighting and quiet of the room, he knew it was night. The pain in his hands was growing more intense, but he refused to push the button that would inject him with another dose of soothing medicinal relief. He earned this pain by losing Gaymer to the Demon Twink.

"Would you like some water or something to eat?" Doug opened his eyes to see it was his beloved Brutus who had asked the question. Brutus leaned forward into the light. His tough and gruff exterior was muted by the orange prison jumpsuit and shackles on his wrist and ankles. "Juan Carlos arranged for me to stay with you," he said with a slight snarl to his voice. "If it hadn't been for him and his meddling heroes, you'd be fine. We'd be married and ruling this city."

Doug reached out with a bandaged hand. "No, it was my own foolishness and pride that caused this."

115

"Don't say that." Brutus carefully took his hand. "You commanded a great pack of Pups. You still do." Brutus lowered his voice.

Doug narrowed his eyes at Brutus. "The pack has been disbanded. Hasn't it?"

"They tried, but our pack bond is too strong." Brutus patted his hand gently. "For now, we only want you to rest and get well."

Doug smiled at the show of love and support. "I will, and then we will do what we can to help rescue Gaymer from the Demon Twink."

"For you, I'll ensure his safe return." Brutus brought Doug's hand up to his lips to kiss. "Then I'll do whatever it takes to make sure you are happy and safe."

Doug smiled at his lover. "I remember making you that very same promise." His smile faltered. "If only I could have kept it."

"You did and then some." Brutus stroked his arm lovingly. "Now it is my turn to return the favor."

Doug covered Brutus' hand with his own. "We'll protect and love each other." He patted Brutus' hand. "Get some rest. You watched over me; now I'll watch over you."

High Tech guided the Shadow Disc down to where Shadow Guardian sat perched on the rooftop. He found it somewhat exhilarating to be out patrolling with his lover, especially on a quiet night when the worst crime they encountered was littering. The idea of being Shadow Guardian's sidekick was becoming much more appealing now that it was becoming a reality.

"Slow night." Shadow Guardian stood and turned to High Tech. "Sorry there's not more action for you."

High Tech stepped off the Shadow Disc. With a wink, he said, "That's okay. I get enough action at home."

"Naughty." Shadow Guardian took High Tech into his arms. "I love how you look in your suit."

High Tech blushed. "It is a bit revealing." He reached up and stroked Shadow Guardian's face. "I was self-conscious about it at first, but when I see how you look at me when I wear it, I feel like the sexiest man alive."

"You are." Shadow Guardian's mask opened to reveal his mouth. "It's all I can do to keep my hands off you when I see you walking around with that big sexy brain of yours." He kissed High Tech.

High Tech rested his head on Shadow Guardian's chest. "You always know the right thing to say." High Tech chuckled. "Most of the time."

"That's why I have you." Shadow Guardian held High Tech tighter to his chest. "You make me a better person."

With a smile in his voice, High Tech said, "We make each other better."

"Wait." Shadow Guardian pulled back from High Tech. "Keagan and Boots. I get it now."

High Tech thought for a moment. Covering his mouth, he gasped. "How did we miss it? It was so obvious."

CHAPTER 14

Dante stepped into the hotel penthouse suite followed by the lone thrall he brought with him. The front desk clerk had raised an eyebrow when he checked in sans luggage and with a handsome muscular man who said nothing as they completed the check in. Her quiet indignation was of little concern for Dante. He needed to stay focused on the plan. His and Finn's plan.

Dante waved his hand, creating a portal back to his home. *Why bother with packing when you simply can have your muscle minions carry it over?* Several of Dante's thralls stepped forth through the portal, carrying his things, followed by Death Drop strutting comically. *I need better help.*

Dante winked at Finn on the other side and smiled when Finn returned the wink as the portal closed. The six thralls carefully put away Dante's things while Death Drop sprawled herself out on the couch and scratched herself.

"Have you heard from Lip-Sync yet?" Dante growled. Death Drop shook her head no then shrugged. Dante let out a sound of frustration. "Why did she have to take vacation now of all times?" Death Drop shrugged. "It was a rhetorical question," Dante chided, turning to observe his muscle minions.

"Tonight, we shall send these lesser muscle minions out to see if we can lure Sentry out for you to capture," Dante reaffirmed their plans as he caressed the face of one of his muscle minions. "I may lose a few of them, but that is something I am willing to risk." He turned to Death Drop. "Remember, we need Sentry alive." Death Drop pouted. "I said alive, not unharmed."

Death Drop grinned, showing her razor-sharp teeth.

Keagan jumped from his desk, and his pink fur armor sprouted when Felipe put his hand on his pensive assistant's shoulder. "A little jumpy?" Felipe asked.

"Sorry." Kegan touched his ring, receding his pink fur. "I know Boots is with Joshua and Fierce, but I'm worried about him."

Felipe nodded his head. "I wish I could tell you that I understand, but your world is completely new to me."

"Me too." Keagan sighed.

Felipe pulled Keagan's chair out for him. "You're in good hands." He let out a little laugh. "You know you're family now, right? We protect our family."

"Family?" Keagan raised an eyebrow. "What do you mean, family?"

Felipe shook his head in amusement. "Exactly that. Family. You can try and fight it, but you got taken in by the greatest group of people I have ever encountered. They'll help you figure everything out."

"I sure hope so." Keagan took his seat. "This connection that Boots and I have is so strange."

Felipe moved around and pulled a chair up to Keagan's desk. "Tell me about it. Maybe I can help."

"Well, when I first met Boots, he didn't know how to talk. Our fingers touched, and we connected mentally. We shared," Keagan tried to find the right words, "ourselves. Our entire lives. I don't know how else to explain it, but it started before then. It was from the moment I saw him that I felt this draw toward him."

Felipe leaned forward. "You were attracted to him?"

"No, it was more than that." Keagan looked off into the distance. "I don't know how to explain it. Fierce is insistent that I have to protect him. Boots is insistent on having to protect me."

Felipe mulled over Keagan's words. "Maybe you're supposed to protect each other?"

"To survive that laboratory, he had to be hard as stone, but with me, his happiness soars." Keagan looked at Filipe. "He'd do anything to protect me, and that scares me. I'm scared he'll do something crazy to protect me."

Felipe gave him a sympathetic look. "One thing I've learned is that you cannot protect people from everything, and sometimes protecting the one you love brings out the best in people."

"I hope you're right, considering the fact he's capable of great good or great evil." Keagan leaned back in his chair, defeated.

Felipe raised an eyebrow. "Wait. What?"

"Make yourselves at home," Doctor Gingerman said, stepping into his penthouse apartment. "I apologize that I haven't been able to get the stench of Demon Twink out of it yet."

Mama Bear entered, sniffing the air. "How much longer must we tolerate them?"

"I like Death Drop." Honey Bear laughed, following her in. "She makes me laugh."

Papa Bear pushed past Honey Bear and eyed the room. "How could you afford a place like this on your DJC salary?"

"DJC was simply a means to an end." Doctor Gingerman went to the bar and began pouring himself a drink. "The Head of the Board and I have been orchestrating things for centuries, waiting for the proper moment to strike." Doctor Gingerman took a sip of his vodka and soda. "In order for that to happen, we need B12 and Teddy back."

Papa Bear snarled, "Why do we need them? The three of us are more than enough for what we need."

"You are not part of the we," Doctor Gingerman corrected him. "You three are elite soldiers, the first of many we need. B12 is the first of the grunt soldiers to be controlled by the chip Gaymer is perfecting for us that we need to fulfill our plans."

Strolling over to the couch, Mama Bear sat down with a flourish. "Come to Mama, boys." Honey Bear immediately went over and took a seat by Mama Bear. "Papa Bear." Mama Bear's voice had a hint of warning.

"Fine." Papa Bear joined her on the couch.

Mama Bear smiled triumphantly. "That's my Papa Bear."

"The three of you make the perfect family," Doctor Gingerman mocked.

Honey Bear snuggled up against Mama Bear. "We do, don't we?"

"Yes, we do." Mama Bear patted Honey Bear on the shoulder. "What is the plan, Doctor Gingerman?"

Doctor Gingerman downed the last of his drink. "Diego Sanz has been looking for me. I have agreed to meet with him at his penthouse apartment. You three will accompany me with your magical disguises. The location spell places our prey there." Doctor Gingerman poured himself another drink. "Make sure you're prepared to strike." He downed half his drink. "Casualties are acceptable."

"Aspen!" Dion shouted as she stormed out of her office. Lowering her voice, she addressed her assistant, "I get it that you're upset about Gaymer, but could you please chill on the cold?"

Looking at her, Aspen asked flatly, "Was that a joke?"

"No," Dion said loud enough so only he could hear. "I'd like to make it through the day without getting frostbite. It's down to forty degrees in here."

Aspen closed his eyes in concentration. The chill in the air slowly faded away. Opening his eyes, he said, "I'll try to control my powers better."

"That's all I ask," Dion said gently. "For us to get Gaymer back, you have to keep a cool head." Aspen cocked his head at her. "No, that wasn't a joke either. Just a poor choice of words."

Aspen exhaled a puff of frozen air. "I feel so useless. Chitter's tracker went dead for so long. Now we have this lead, and I still have to sit here and be patient instead of mounting some grand rescue."

"You're taking care of Chitter for him." Dion put her hand on his but yanked it back when she felt the bitter cold. "Boy, could you defrost a bit?"

Aspen flexed his fingers. "Sorry. My emotions directly affect my powers."

"I know." Dion winked at Aspen. "What do you say we grab some marshmallows and go talk to Aiden about Doctor Tyson?"

Aspen's body warmed with amusement. "You know he hates it when we roast marshmallows over his hair."

"I know. I also know you keep a bag of marshmallows in your desk." Dion opened the top drawer of Aspen's desk and pulled out the bag of marshmallows. "What do you say?"

Laughing, Aspen stood. "I say that Diego has been a bad influence on us both."

"What does this mean?" Juan Carlos asked, motioning to the screen displaying the ley line convergence.

Alex shrugged. "This is out of my knowledge base."

"It means we need to do a deep mystical investigation of DJC Corporate offices." Esmerelda's voice came over the speaker in Alex's office.

Hand on his chin, Doctor Tyson stepped forward to study the screen. "We're missing something. Something painfully obvious. A common denominator."

"We could look at all the cross points and see if there is any correlation." Alex tapped on the controls, putting green circles around all of the other points. "Let me send this over to our mischievous trio and see what they come up with."

"Is that what we're calling them?" Juan Carlos asked with a smile. "Considering I found them huddled together talking quietly this morning, it seems appropriate."

Alex added, "I also caught them looking over the Shadow Guardian and Sentry suit schematics ... with Diego."

"*Ay, Dios mío!*" Esmerelda gasped.

Juan Carlos began rubbing his forehead. "Maybe I should check in with Joshua."

"Hold that thought," Esmerelda cut in then went silent. "Freddy picked up the scent of the Demon Twink... The one I vanquished."

Juan Carlos nodded. "Finn Andrews." He snapped his fingers. "He got married shortly after his father died."

"He must have had a deep bond with someone on this plane that would have kept him from being sent to the Hell dimensions," Esmerelda thought aloud. "A second demon twink."

Alex began typing on the console. "His husband took over Andrews Industries." A picture of Dante appeared on the screen. "We should get

Aiden or Aspen in here to confirm if this is the guy they fought." Aiden burst into the room, blocking the door with his body.

"Aiden?" Doctor Tyson went over to his boyfriend. "Are you okay?"

Aiden pointed at the screen. "Hey! That's the arrogant Demon Twink we fought!"

"That confirms it," Esmerelda commented over the speaker. "We're dealing with two demon twinks."

Doctor Tyson examined his boyfriend. "What is that white stuff all over you?"

"Marshmallow." Aiden took several deep breaths then hugged his man. "Dion and Aspen were using my hair to roast marshmallows."

Alex coughed in his hand to hide his laughter. "I'll get Diego to make them stop."

"He's the one that gave them the sticks to roast the marshmallows on," Aiden responded.

"Should we be worried that we haven't seen Fierce, Alegro, and Chitter all day?" Boots asked, sitting down on Joshua's bed.

Half listening, Joshua opened his closet and scanned his wardrobe. "I'm sure they are fine off playing together somewhere." Joshua pulled out a black blazer with gold trim.

"I like it." Boots cocked his head. "What's it for?"

Joshua laid the jacket on the bed. He stared at it while answering, "I have this sort of date thing tonight."

"What's a date thing?" Boots asked, curiously.

Joshua looked at Boots in disbelief then remembered his situation. "Oh, sorry. A date is something two people go on to get to know each other," he bit the side of his lip, "to see if they want to see each other romantically."

"Why is it sort of a date?" Boots asked.

Joshua went to his dresser. Pulling out a black V-neck tee and a white one, he held them up for Boots. "Because they kidnapped my boyfriend and tried to kill me once or twice."

"You have a boyfriend, and you're going out on a date with the person who kidnapped them?" Boots asked, trying to understand. "That doesn't make sense."

Joshua laid the black shirt on the suit jacket. "On the surface it doesn't." He laughed. "I have two boyfriends. I'm in a poly relationship with Teddy and Jack. You'll meet them eventually. As for Lip-Sync, well, that's complicated. Aiden is the only one that knows besides you that I'm going out with her."

"What if she tries to kidnap you?" Boots asked, a hint of fear in his voice.

Joshua returned to his closet and pulled out a pair of khaki pants. "That means you'll have to learn to dodge better and stop dropping your right." He turned and winked at Boots. "You did really well in training today. I didn't expect you to pick up on all those moves so fast."

"I want to protect Keagan the way he protects me," Boots said with a blush.

Joshua sat down beside Boots on the bed. "He really means a lot to you, doesn't he?"

"He does." Boots looked off into the distance. "From the moment I escaped that laboratory, I felt I was being guided somewhere, and then I saw him." Boots' face brightened. "He's so adorable and confident and sweet and kind and brave and selfless." Boots looked over at Joshua with a smile. "I know Demona says that I am capable of great evil or great good, but when I'm with him, all I want to be is good."

Joshua put an arm around Boots. "It sounds like you're in love."

"Is that what love is?" Boots scratched his head. "Is that the reason I want to touch him in his underwear area?"

Joshua's chest heaved with laughter. "That's lust, and I'm pretty sure he wants to do that to you too, but try kissing first. Okay?"

"Okay." Boots smiled. "I'll kiss him in his underwear area first."

CHAPTER 15

"BOOTS!" KEAGAN TACKLED Boots into a hug as soon as he opened the door.

Burying his face into Keagan's shoulder, Boots returned the hug. "I missed you too." Their bodies relaxed into each other. "We got all your stuff moved into your apartment this morning." Ashamed, Boots pulled away. "I put your stuff away. I didn't have anything to put away."

"Our apartment." Keagan brushed Boots' cheek with his fingertips. "Felipe gave me the day off tomorrow. I say we spend the day getting you things to go in our apartment."

Boots smiled warmly. "All I need is Fierce and you." He winked at Keagan. "I guess clothes that fit would be nice. If I keep wearing yours, neither of us is going to have anything to wear."

Keagan laughed. "Let's get Fierce and go home." He looked over Boots' shoulder. "Where is Fierce? Isn't Joshua supposed to be here with you?"

Taking Keagan by the hand, he led him toward the rooftop garden. "Fierce is building a tree fort with Alegro and Chitter. Joshua left for his date." His voice grew bashful. "Do you think we could go out on a date sometime?"

"Um, sure." Uncomfortable, Keagan pulled at the collar of his shirt. "You do know what a date is, right?"

Boots opened the door to the garden. "Yeah, it's where you go out with someone who has tried to kill you and see if you have a romantic connection." Boots thought for a second. "I think one of the people on the date is supposed to kidnap the other's boyfriend." Boots' face brightened. "Oh, and if it goes well, you get to touch each other in their underwear area!"

"What in the world did they teach you here?" Keagan asked, stunned. "Let's get Fierce and go home."

"Why won't you tell me what you were helping the mischievous trio with?" Alex asked, stepping into their apartment.

Diego rolled his eyes. "I told you. They wanted to know how to build a tree fort."

"You're really going with that story?" Alex grumbled. "You know I'm going to find out."

Diego grinned smugly. "You're going to love it when you do." He put his arm around Alex. "In the meantime, let's get ready for Doctor Gingerman's visit. He should be here in the next fifteen minutes. Let's make sure we're ready. I find it very suspicious that he suddenly contacted us when we haven't been able to find him."

"Right. Aspen and Aiden are in Shadow Command in case anything happens. Juan Carlos and Aaron are out to dinner with Felipe. Keagan and Boots should be at their place by now," Alex listed off. "We need to get Chitter and Alegro into Shadow Command, and Joshua is out on his date." Alex winced. "I wasn't supposed to tell you that last part."

Diego's face brightened. "Joshua is out on a date? Who is it with? When do we get to meet them?" He paused. "Wait. What about his relationship with Jack and Teddy?"

"Yes," Alex said with a huff. "I don't know. No, we don't, and I don't know."

Diego pouted. "I want to meet his date."

"You're not meeting his date." Aiden's voice came through their coms. "We have a problem.

Keagan and Boots are in the garden trying to find the mischievous trio."

"And Doctor Gingerman just arrived with three bodyguards," Aspen added.

Diego looked at Alex. "We were expecting him alone."

"Okay, we can work with this." Alex thought for a moment. "We'll keep them in here while Aiden or Aspen get the others into Shadow Command."

Diego nodded. "You have your High Tech suit ready, right?"

"Yes, daddy, and I'm wearing clean under-wear." Alex patted him on the chest.

Diego smirked. "You're wearing underwear?"

"Guys, focus." Aspen's stern voice came over the coms. "We lost the elevator feed. I think I saw Gingerman put something on the elevator when he pushed the button." The lights in the apart-ment flickered. Aspen's staticky voice came over the coms. "Aiden can't get the doors..."

Alex looked at Diego. "*Mierda.*"

"I'll meet with Doctor Gingerman. You go into the garden and make sure everyone stays safe." The door chime drew their attention. Diego pulled Alex into a kiss. "Be safe."

Alex returned the kiss. "You too." He rushed out into the garden, his clothes morphing into his High Tech suit.

"Coming!" Diego shouted when the door chimed again. Heading to the door, he adjusted his tie and put on his best fake smile. Opening the door, Diego exclaimed merrily, "Doctor Gingerman! You're early! And you brought company! Come in! Come in!"

The redheaded man forced an unconvincing smile. "I apologize, but we were expecting more traffic." Doctor Gingerman stepped forward. "I hope you don't mind, but I brought my security team."

"I was unaware our meeting required a security team. Should I summon mine?" Diego half joked, stepping aside to allow them entry. "I can have them up here in a jiffy."

Doctor Gingerman smiled maliciously at Diego. "No, no. I didn't feel leaving them in the car with the window cracked was appropriate."

"No, no. We wouldn't want that." Diego led them into the living room. "Come sit. I assume they are cleared to discuss delicate matters and are under the appropriate NDAs."

"Of course!" Doctor Gingerman took a seat on the couch facing the garden, and the disguised Bears stood stoically behind him. "I was hoping to see Juan Carlos or that adorable boyfriend of yours. What is his name? Alex?"

"Juan Carlos is having dinner with his son and fiancé," Diego said sweetly. "Alex is babysitting some mischievous youngsters."

Doctor Gingerman gave a slight look to the man standing on his right. Diego saw the almost imperceptible nod of confirmation. "Well, let's get down to business, shall we? I believe you had some questions about the hypnotic box that you shelved?"

"Yes, but may I ask where you have been?" Diego took a seat that deliberately blocked Doctor Gingerman's view of the garden. "We have been looking for you for quite some time, and now here you are, contacting us."

Doctor Gingerman let out a soft chuckle. "I am not inclined to reveal that." Diego saw the man on Doctor Gingerman's left shift uneasily. The one on the right started fidgeting. The one in the middle elbowed them both at the same time. "Now, to the matter at hand, what questions do you have about the hypnotic box?"

"When I shelved it, I removed the hard drive and the motherboard, making it nothing more than a fancy box, but a working version of that box was being used by Doug Trainer, and then later, a smaller version was developed." Diego leaned forward. "Do you have any idea how they could have gotten the programming? Your programming?"

Doctor Gingerman glanced up at the guard directly behind him then gave Diego a sinister smile. "I won't insult your intelligence. We both know I orchestrated the liberation of my box and provided the necessary parts and programming before giving it to Doug Trainer." Doctor Gingerman made a flippant gesture. "The Pup Uprising would have happened a lot sooner had you been a dear and left it alone."

"Then you are working for the Demon Twink!" Diego accused, jumping to his feet. He looked down for a split second, feeling the floor below him beginning to warm. He smiled.

"I work *with* them, not for them." Doctor Gingerman snapped his fingers. The security detail behind him flickered then revealed themselves to be the Three Bears. "Now be a dear and fetch me my property. I promise your death will be quick and painless if you cooperate," Doctor Gingerman leaned forward, "Shadow Guardian."

Diego tapped his chest, transforming him into Shadow Guardian. "No point in denying it now." He took a fighting stance. "I don't know what property you think I have of yours, but you're not getting it."

"Experiment B12. Where is he?" Papa Bear snarled.

138

Doctor Gingerman leaned back. "We know he's here."

"Even if he was here, I'd never give him to you," Shadow Guardian proclaimed.

Doctor Gingerman sighed. "Papa Bear, do your thing."

"Gladly!" Papa Bear exclaimed with menacing glee.

Papa Bear launched himself over the couch at Shadow Guardian. Shadow Guardian fell back onto the couch and thrust his legs up, jamming his feet into Papa Bear's chest. The couch flipped back, causing Shadow Guardian's kick to send Papa Bear hurling toward the glass wall to the garden.

"Ugh! Diego and his firesafe building!" Fire growled, aiming her concentrated heat blast at the ceiling.

Aspen thought for a moment. "Stop. You're only going to wear yourself out."

"How are we going to get out of here?" Fire asked, wiping the sweat from her brow.

Aspen's fingertips glowed blue then traveled over his body to transform him into Ice. "We work together."

"Like we did with the Demon Twink? Well, one of them." Fire thought for a moment. "Isn't it redundant to say demon and twink? I mean, aren't all twinks demons?"

Ice shook her head in dismay. "You do realize we are twinks, right?"

"Yeah, but we're not demons." Realization hit Fire. "Oh! Point taken. Okay, let's do this."

Ice took Fire's hand. "The difference in temperature should confuse the fire suppression system enough to let us break through the ceiling."

"Ice fire," Fire said merrily, pointing their joined hands to the ceiling. "Let's do this."

Fire and ice swirled from their joined hands and hit the ceiling. "It's working! It can't dissipate the heat and the cold at the same time!"

"Keagan! Boots!" High Tech called to the two young men staring up into a tree. Coming up to them, he asked, "Where are Alegro, Chitter, and Fierce?"

Boots pointed up into the tree. "They won't come out of their tree fort."

"What are you wearing?" Keagan asked, eyeing High Tech's skimpy uniform. "A little on the skimpy side, isn't it?"

"Diego designed it," High Tech answered. "You guys aren't supposed to be here." He looked up into the tree. "And you three need to get down here. We have to get you all someplace safe."

At the mention of danger, pink magic swirled around Keagan. Pink fur, ears, and tail replaced his work attire. In his left hand appeared his baton. His eyes, pupils narrowed to that like a cat's, flashed pink. "What's going on?"

"Doctor Gingerman—"

Boots cut him off with a fearful shriek. "Doctor Gingerman! He wants to take me back to the laboratory!" He clung to Kitty Boy. "Please, don't let him take me."

"No one is taking you away from me." Kitty Boy protectively pulled him close. "Stay here with Fierce, Chitter, and Alegro. The glorified go-go boy and I will protect you."

"Hey!" High Tech shouted a moment before they heard the sound of glass shattering.

Chitter stuck their head out of the fort. "Coms are down. Alegro can't call for help." Chitter twitched their whiskers. "What do you want us to do?"

"Hide," High Tech ordered. "Come on, Kitty Boy."

Watching the two rush away, Chitter twitched their whiskers again. "That's not going to happen."

"Fierce? Chitter? Alegro?" Boots called up. "Where should we go?"

Fierce leapt down out of the tree. "Meow."

"Fight? Are you crazy?" Boots looked at the kitten incredulously.

Fierce jumped up and tapped the center of Boots' chest, transforming his clothing into the hot pink and green battle uniform Aiden designed for him. Fierce let out a seductive "Meow."

"Flirt after the fight," Chitter scolded, leaping out onto one of the branches, followed by Alegro. "Alegro and I are going to attack from the trees. You keep him safe."

Boots looked at Chitter then to Fierce. "He's a kitten. How is he supposed to do that?"

"Meow," Fierce answered, turning and facing the sound of the fight.

Chitter and Alegro moved along the branches toward the battle. Chitter called back, "He's bigger and more powerful than he looks!"

"Who is there?" Boots asked, jumping at the sound of a snapping twig off to the side.

Fierce turned and hissed at the approaching shadow. "Meow!"

"Papa Bear," High Tech said under his breath when he saw the muscled brute standing in the shattered remains of the glass wall. He raised both arms, a clear visor appearing over his eyes. Targeting marks appeared before him. "He's going to regret coming into our home."

From High Tech's wrists shot four black round balls, hitting Papa Bear in the back with a splatter. A moment later, they released their electric charge, causing Papa Bear to scream in angry pain. Shadow Guardian came hurling through the broken wall to land a flying kick into Papa Bear's chest, sending him crashing back onto the ground.

"Is everyone safe?" Shadow Guardian asked, rushing up to High Tech and Kitty Boy.

Kitty Boy growled. "They aren't."

"Look! They have a kitty!" Honey Bear shouted gleefully as he and Mama Bear stepped out into the garden. His eyes went wild and his voice went sinister. "I want to play with the kitty."

"Let's play." The ends of Kitty Boy's baton transformed into cat paws. "This kitty has claws." Razor-sharp nails sprang from the paws.

Mama Bear helped Papa Bear up. "You go and play with the kitty. Papa will handle that rude Shadow Guardian, and I guess that leaves the go-go boy to me."

"You modeled my uniform after a go-go boy, didn't you?" High Tech accused.

Shadow Guardian shrugged. "Actually, after one of Freddy's costumes from when he used to dance."

"Guys!" Kitty Boy snarled. "Bad guys!"

Returning his focus to the Three Bears, High Tech griped, "Fine. I'll take on the Drag Queen Bear."

"Diego Sanz," Papa Bear snarled, brushing the glass from his hairy body, "or do you prefer Shadow Guardian?" He touched the bracelets on his wrists. They glowed then extended forward to cover his hands, forming bear paws with razor-sharp claws. "How do you like my new and improved bear claws?"

Shadow Guardian stood straight. Tapping his chin in thought, he said, "They don't really go with your shoes."

"Wait? What?" Papa Bear looked down at his feet.

Shadow Guardian took advantage of the distraction. He hurled multiple Shadow Stars at Papa Bear as he darted to the left. Mama Bear pulled her string pearls off her neck. In her hands, it grew to four feet long, allowing her to whip it about to deflect Shadow Guardian's attack.

Taking advantage of the opportunity, High Tech shot multiple black orbs at Honey Bear. Mama Bear tried to deflect them with her pearls, but these exploded on impact into huge plumes of smoke that engulfed the Three Bears.

From the smoke came honey amber spheres flying at them. With his cat-like reflexes, Kitty Boy moved in front of them. Twirling his baton at rapid speed, he diverted them away to spatter harmlessly into the ground. Mama Bear's pearls came flying out of the smoke to tangle in the baton and his wrists, stopping his twirling.

Red eyes glowed in the smoke. Mama Bear stepped out of the smoke. "Bad kitty."

She yanked her pearls back, pulling Kitty Boy toward her. Using the momentum of her attack, he pushed off the ground toward her, giving him the slack he needed to free his hands and baton. With his hands free, he attached his baton to his thigh and extended his claws.

"I don't like your cat-itude." Kitty Boy sank his claws into Mama Bear's beehive wig. He pulled at her cotton candy textured hair. "You should be ashamed of yourself." His tail whipped around to smack her in the face. "Your hair is a cat-astrophy."

Kitty Boy dodged Mama Bear's attempts to pull him off her head. She screeched, "You filthy, vile creature! You'll be declawed when I'm done with you!"

Papa Bear charged out of the smoke, claws extended, toward Shadow Guardian. "I'm going to carve you up like a turkey!"

"That means the go-go boy is mine!" The smoke cleared to reveal Honey Bear, left hand extended toward High Tech. A tube from a canister on his back wrapped around his arm to a blaster on his wrist. Several more honey amber spheres exploded from his wrist. "Let's see your dance moves when you can't move!"

Shadow Guardian twirled at the last moment to avoid Papa Bear's attack, sending him crashing into a tree. "Olé!" With a hand on his hip and one in the air, he looked at Papa Bear. "Didn't we do this dance already?"

"I am not a go-go boy!" High Tech raised his left hand. An invisible barrier similar to Sentry's shield formed. He curved it so when Honey Bear's spheres hit it, they were sent flying back at him instead of exploding. Honey Bear yelped as he dodged the return attack. "My name is High Tech!"

"Yeow!" Kitty Boy cried when Mama Bear finally caught his whipping tail and yanked him from her wig.

Mama Bear twirled him by his tail. "Pink is not your color!" She sent him flying toward Shadow Guardian.

"You arrogant man-child!" Papa Bear snapped, pulling himself from the broken branches and splintered trunk.

"Juan Carlos is going to be pissed you hurt one of his plants." He caught sight of a pink fur ball hurtling toward him. "Say hello to my little kitty."

Shadow Guardian grabbed flying Kitty Boy by the wrists. Using the momentum of Mama Bear's throw, he spun Kitty Boy around then released him at Papa Bear. Kitty Boy's feet slammed into Papa Bear, sending him stumbling back into the broken tree. Using Papa Bear's chest as a spring board, he did a flip in the air to land in a crouch beside Shadow Guardian.

"Didn't you hear?" Kitty Boy stood. "I'm the cat's meow."

Shadow Guardian tapped on Kitty Boy's shoulder. "That was bad, and that's coming from me."

"Can I get a little help over here?!" High Tech shouted, holding up both hands to keep his protective shield against Honey Bear's blasts and Mama Bear's pearl whips.

Honey Bear laughed maniacally. "His shield is weakening."

147

"Use your go-go boy powers!" Shadow Guardian shouted, kicking Papa Bear in the face and knocking him out. Taking off running toward Mama Bear and Honey Bear, he threw several Shadow Stars at them.

High Tech shouted back, "Not funny!" High Tech concentrated. Two tendrils rose from his shoulders over his protective barrier. "Let's see if they like this." He shot multiple black balls at Mama Bear and Honey Bear.

"I don't like balls flying at my face!" Mama Bear whipped her pearls about, knocking High Tech's barrage off to the side. She did a quick split, letting the Shadow Stars slice into her hair. Standing back up, she snarled, "You all are going to pay to have my hair done!"

"Oh, honey, they are doing you a favor by wrecking that out-of-date style," Ice said, stepping through the broken glass wall with Fire.

Fire waved her hand as she spoke, flames dancing from her fingers. "Which one of you thought it was cute to lock us up in our own home?"

"Get back, you crazy kitten!" Doctor Gingerman shouted, backing into the battle with an arm around Boots' throat. "One more step and I'll hurt him."

Fierce hissed, "Meow!"

"Boots!" Kitty Boy took off running toward the two.

Recovering, Papa Bear snatched Kitty Boy by his tail. "Filthy alley cat!" He whipped Kitty Boy back and up in the air. "Let's see if you land on your feet from this height."

"Keagan!" Boots slammed the back of his head into Doctor Gingerman's face then jammed his booted foot down on Doctor Gingerman's foot. He then hurled Doctor Gingerman over his shoulder toward Fierce. "I'll save you!" He took off running across the garden, knocking Honey Bear and Mama Bear out of the way when they tried to stop him.

Papa Bear stood ready, blocking his path. "Come on, freak. I can take you."

Boots ducked as he ran. He slammed into Papa Bear's midsection. He stood, lifting Papa Bear up off his feet and tossing Papa Bear behind him before diving over the edge after Kitty Boy.

"Boots!" High Tech shouted.

Shadow Guardian started after the pair but was met with a furious Papa Bear. "Where do you think you're going?"

"Out of the way!!" Ice froze the ground under Papa Bear.

Fire hit him in the face with a fireball that caused him to slip and fall on his butt. "He has people to rescue."

"Meow!" Fierce leapt up on the fallen Doctor Gingerman's face and began clawing him.

Several of Honey Bear's orbs hit Fire and Ice, covering them in the sticky, amber honey liquid. "Stay out of this!"

"Really?" Fire raised her body temperature, melting Honey Bear's attack.

Ice lowered her body temperature, causing the honey liquid to freeze, crack, and break. "They are making me miss Death Drop and Lip-Sync." She sent a blast of ice at Honey Bear.

Honey Bear jumped out of the way of Ice's blast, allowing the blast to hit Mama Bear while she tried to pull the Shadow Stars from her wig. She was encapsulated in a block of ice. Her eyes glowed red through the ice. The ice shattered, freeing Mama Bear and sending ice shards all over.

"Get back here!" Papa Bear grabbed Shadow Guardian by the ankle and slung him back toward the battle.

Shadow Guardian caught a glimpse of Chitter in a tree with Alegro. Landing, he said, "Chitter! Nut all over him!"

Everyone grew silent. Chitter stuck their head out of the tree. "That is not appropriate battle banter."

"What the..." Ice shook her head.

Fire threw up her hands. "Yeah, I'm not taking any part of that."

"Dude, what is wrong with you?" Papa Bear asked, wide-eyed and sounding a little scared.

Shadow Guardian held up placating hands. "Poor choice of words. I'm sorry."

"Apology accepted," Chitter chirped happily. "Now, let's get squirrely." Chitter began hurling acorns at Papa Bear that exploded on impact. "Now go save our boys!"

Shadow Guardian ran to the edge of the roof and was about to jump over when a glowing pink light nearly blinded him. Shielding his eyes, he staggered back. Under his mask, he smiled up at what was causing the light. "Look! It happened!"

Kitty Boy fumbled for his baton as he fell down the side to the building. He tried shooting a grappler up to catch the side of the building, but it fell short of its target. *I really hope that cats have nine lives.* Kitty Boy retracted the grappler. He turned one of the ends into a cat claw and tried to sink it into the building wall but only succeeded in creating sparks.

"Keagan!" He heard Boots call his name from up above.

He made out a figure hurling toward him at rocket speed. "That crazy fool."

"Keagan!" Boots grabbed him as he passed and pulled him into his arms. "I'll save you!"

Holding onto Boots, Kitty Boy asked, "And who is going to save you?"

"I ... I don't know." Boots squeezed him tighter. "I just knew I had to jump after you."

Kitty Boy caressed Boots' face. "Well, if this is the end of our story, I'm not letting it end without giving you a kiss."

Kitty Boy kissed Boots. Pink swirls of magic surrounded them. The rushing air around them slowed. Kitty Boy could hear the sound of flapping wings but ignored it. He felt the truth in their kiss, what everyone else had seen but they hadn't. He knew the secret Fierce was hiding from them.

"Keagan," Boots whispered into the kiss, "we're flying."

Eyes still closed, enjoying the last brief moments he had with Boots, Kitty Boy said, "No, we're falling. It just feels like we're flying."

"No, really." Boots pulled back from the kiss. "I have wings and we're flying."

Kitty Boy opened his eyes to see two huge bat-style wings protruding out of Boots' back, flapping. "What in the world?"

"Am I a demon?" Boots asked curiously. "I don't feel like a demon."

Kitty Boy marveled at Boots' wings. "I don't think so." He looked up at the rooftop above. "Do you think you could get us back up to the roof?"

"Hold onto your whiskers." Boots began flapping his wings.

The two rose back up, gradually picking up speed. Boots looked at a smiling Kitty Boy. He kissed Kitty Boy again. Magical light surrounded them and cast the city below them in a pink hue. They shot up past the roof. The light around them faded when they stopped the kiss.

Wings flapping, Boots kept them hovering over the rooftop garden. "Later, can we touch each other in our underwear places?"

"Let's kick some butt first." Kitty Boy kissed Boots on the cheek. "Catch you on the ground."

Kitty Boy jumped from Boots' arms toward the rooftop. He landed feet first on top of Papa Bear's head, causing him to slip again on the frozen ground. Pushing off Papa Bear, he twirled in the air to land in a crouch in front of Mama Bear and Honey Bear.

Boots did a loop in the air and landed gently beside him. "Wings are cool!"

"Meow!" Fierce said excitedly, swiping one last time at Doctor Gingerman's face before dashing off to stand beside Boots and Kitty Boy.

"Surrender!" Shadow Guardian tossed an unconscious Papa Bear at Mama Bear's feet.

Chitter and Alegro came rushing up beside Shadow Guardian. "Don't make us get squirrely again."

Mama Bear looked at the fallen Papa Bear and Doctor Gingerman. Honey Bear wildly shot about at the gathering heroes that were surrounding them. "This did not go as planned." She touched her bracelet.

Black magic dripped up from the ground around them and Doctor Gingerman. They sank down. Into the magic. "Until we meet again." Honey Bear cackled.

Chitter and Alegro rushed up over Boots while Fierce jumped up into Kitty Boy's arms. "You look good with wings," Chitter squawked merrily. They examined his wings. "What are you?"

Alegro vibrated.

"It is not rude in this case," Chitter rebutted.

"What he is ... is mine." Kitty Boy put an arm around Boots.

Proudly, Fierce said, "Meow."

"Fine. Ours," Kitty Boy relented. "It is a good question, though. Are you a demon or not?"

Fierce answered, "Meow."

"I'm sort of a gargoyle?" Boots looked to Kitty Boy. "What is a gargoyle?"

Shadow Guardian put a hand on Kitty Boy's shoulder. "We'll have Demona explain it to us later. In the meantime, we should make sure that everyone else is safe."

"About that." Fire fidgeted. "I guess I should tell you who Joshua's date is."

CHAPTER 16

"CAN I INTEREST YOU IN SOME-thing from our wine list?" the waiter asked Joshua.

Joshua smiled uncomfortably. "Water is fine, thank you." He didn't miss the disappointment in the waiter's face before he turned and left. *I can't risk any impairment in case this is a trap,* Joshua reasoned.

Suspicious, he covertly scanned the restaurant for any signs of danger. He scrutinized every patron, every member of the staff. *Lip-Sync could be any of them.*

"I'm glad you came." Joshua sprang to his feet, knocking into their waiter, causing the man to spill the water all over himself.

Joshua snatched a napkin off the table, sending the silverware on it flying. "I'm sorry!"

"You stabbed me!" the waiter shrieked in pain.

Joshua looked down to see a fork sticking out of the waiter's thigh. "Oh my!"

"Allow me." The man who surprised Joshua went to the hysterical waiter. Covering the waiter's mouth with one hand, he yanked the fork out. The waiter screeched into the man's hand. Dropping the fork on the table, he removed his hand from the waiter's mouth.

"I assume you'd prefer not to serve us." The man smiled, amusement in his voice. "For your own safety."

Crying, the waiter began to blubber. "I just got out of therapy from that incident with Diego Sanz last year!"

The man patted the waiter on the head. "You go tell your boss you need a mental health week and go home."

"My therapist is never going to believe this," the waiter sniffled, walking away.

"I stabbed the waiter." Joshua sank back into his chair, embarrassed. "With a fork."

The man put a hand on Joshua's shoulder. "At least you got the first date stabbing out of the way."

"First date stabbing?" Joshua looked up at the man. He knew the handsome man with chestnut brown hair parted to the left, wearing an eye patch that a white scar ran under and down his cheek. "Lip-Sync?"

He winked at Joshua. "You can call me Corey out of Drag." He looked around at everyone staring and whispering at them. "Perhaps we should find someplace else to dine? Maybe someplace where you haven't injured the wait staff?"

"This was a bad idea." Joshua stood. "I should go."

Corey put a hand on his shoulder. "Please, don't go. Just because I've kicked your ass a couple of times doesn't mean we can't have a nice dinner."

"You bested me one time." Joshua puffed out his chest. "I would have won that last one had your Demon Twink master not threatened to harm Gaymer."

Corey winked at Joshua. "You know I had you."

"Why am I even here?" Joshua growled, annoyed.

Corey smirked. "To cause a scene? Accidently stab a waiter? To get to know me and help me enjoy my last night on vacation?"

"Demon assassins get vacations?" Joshua asked, louder than he intended.

Looking around, Corey suggested, "I think we should take this conversation elsewhere. We're drawing a bit of attention."

"I'm going home." Joshua put his jacket on and started toward the door.

Catching up to Joshua and putting his arm through his, Corey said, "I'm not normally that quick on a first date, but who knows when we'll get a second date."

"You're not coming home with me," Joshua snarled under his breath, stepping into the street.

Coyly, Corey said, "I hope you don't expect to go to my place. I'm not that type of girl."

"You're not any type of girl." Joshua stopped and looked at him. "Or are you?" He let out a sound of annoyance and started walking again. "Never mind. I don't care."

Keeping his arm locked with Joshua's, Corey fell into step with him. "I am a male. I am also a Drag Queen, hence the name Lip-Sync. The rest of my sordid history is quite complicated, and I'll save it for the second date."

"There isn't going to be a second date. There shouldn't have been a first date," Joshua snapped. "I just want to go home and forget this night ever happened."

Corey laughed. "You do know you live in the opposite direction, right?"

"Yes." Joshua stopped and looked around. "Now."

Corey tugged Joshua along. "Come on. Show a girl a fun night out. Let's go to In Between, eat bar food, have sparkling drinks that make us giggle, and enjoy each other's company."

"Why should I go there with you?" Joshua grumbled, allowing himself to be led.

Corey patted Joshua's arm with his other hand. "Because I asked you to. Because there you can let your guard down and show a girl a good time because of the neutrality rules."

"Fine," Joshua said with a hint of smile in his voice. "But I'm not letting my guard down."

Corey leaned his head onto Joshua's shoulder. "So tell me, Joshua, how would you like to have me tonight?"

"Excuse me?" Joshua sputtered.

Corey chuckled. "I mean, do you prefer me as a boy? As a girl? Neither? Something in between?" Corey made his voice seductive when he said, "I'm very versatile."

"Oh, um," Joshua managed to get out, "do whatever makes you feel comfortable."

Corey patted his arm. "Boy it is." They walked arm in arm in silence for a bit. "This is nice. I don't get many chances to go out on a date."

"I guess kidnapping and trying to kill people doesn't give you much time to date," Joshua commented snidely.

Corey sighed. "You flirt your way. I'll flirt mine." His lips curled into a sly smile. "It's not like I caused an innocent waiter trauma by accidently drenching him in water then stabbing him with a fork or anything."

"Can we not mention that again?" Joshua groaned. With a huff, he asked, "Why don't you tell me something about yourself? How did you become a demon assassin?"

Corey thought for a moment. "Once upon a time—"

"Seriously?" Joshua asked, stopping.

Corey ignored his comment and tugged Joshua along. He began again, "Once upon a time, there was a majestic Drag Queen. Her beauty and talent were admired by all. One night, as she made her way back home to her castle, villainous scoundrels attacked her, leaving her near death on the cold, cruel streets."

Corey took in a sharp breath. "In those last moments, the bright light that was her soul darkened from the anger and rage that filled her at what the men had done to her, and she vowed with her dying breath to seek revenge on each of them." He patted Joshua's arm. "Those who say Hell hath no fury like a woman scorned have never seen a pissed off Drag Queen."

Corey continued before Joshua could respond. "A young demon, only a few hundred years or so old, was drawn toward the power of her hate and anger. He offered her the means to carry out her revenge, and in exchange, the Drag Queen would owe him a soul debt, and she would have to sacrifice her beauty."

Joshua tried to stop them, but Corey tugged them on. "She agreed, and before morning, the Drag Queen brought the young demon all ten of the scoundrels' mortal souls to feast upon." Corey shrugged. "My soul debt was fulfilled with Gaymer's kidnapping, but Dante still owns my beauty."

"How can he own your beauty?" Joshua asked, a bit taken aback by the entire story.

Corey tapped his eye patch. "Beauty is in the eye of the beholder." He let out a laugh at Joshua's shocked expression. "It's okay. In exchange for my beauty, I was given the power to shape-shift."

"The lip stick," Joshua said matter-of-factly.

Corey stopped and looked at him. "No. Murderous Red just happens to look good on me, and shape-shifting can leave my lips chapped."

"Wait." Joshua closed his eyes in thought. "You fought me for an ordinary tube of lipstick?"

"Men!" Corey tugged him along. "It wasn't an ordinary tube of lipstick. It was my shade, and the line has been discontinued. I only recently found a shade that remotely matches it."

Joshua laughed. "I stand corrected. I am sorry."

"Apology accepted." Corey put his head back on Joshua's shoulder.

They both stopped at the sound of gunfire and people screaming behind them. Joshua stiffened. With a sigh, Corey looked over at him. "You want to investigate that, don't you?"

"No," Joshua lied, his body tense and ready to jump into action.

"Liar." Corey patted his arm. "You're wearing your suit under your clothes, aren't you?"

Guiltily, Joshua answered, "Yes," then added, "but only because I was going out on a date with you."

"You were expecting a little combat foreplay?" Corey teased.

Joshua blustered out, "No, I mean I expected combat but not foreplay."

"Sure," Corey teased. He patted Joshua on the chest. "Shall we find a safe place to change?"

Joshua shook his head. "No, I'll just alert the others." He activated his com. "That's strange. The coms are down."

"Guess it's up to us." Corey ushered Joshua into a nearby alley. "Change in here, and I'll stand guard."

Joshua pulled off his jacket. "What am I going to do with my clothes?"

"Take them off?" Corey tossed a small, magical, black velvet bag to Joshua. "Put them in there." Another gunshot echoed, followed by more screaming. "Hurry."

A few minutes later, Sentry stepped out of the alleyway. Handing Corey back the small bag, he said, "I'm sorry to cut our date short." He kissed Corey on the cheek then took off running toward the screams.

"Does he really think this date is over?" Corey applied his lipstick. "We haven't had dinner yet."

Sentry rushed back down the street that he and Corey came down, dodging the people running away from the danger. He mentally cursed when he stopped in front of the source of the commotion. It was the restaurant where he had doused the waiter in water before accidently stabbing him with a fork.

"Why me?" the waiter cried inside. "I was going home!"

Sentry peered around the corner through the destroyed front door to see six men holding the staff and patrons at gunpoint. The poor waiter was on his knees with Death Drop making horrid faces at him. Sentry was about to storm in when a delicate hand on his shoulder stopped him. He looked over to see Lip-Sync at his side.

"Dante's muscle minions and Death Drop," Lip-Sync said softly. "It has to be some sort of trap."

Sentry sneered at her. "Is that why you wanted a date with me? To lure me into a trap?"

"No," Lip-Sync said, hurt by the hardness of his words. "I took you away from here, remember?"

Sentry didn't want to, but he believed her. "The others aren't answering, and I can't leave those people in there at Death Drop's mercy."

"And I can't help you." Lip-Sync then added softly, "At least I can't be seen helping you."

Sentry turned to look at her, but she was gone. "Guess I'm on my own." He strode through the front door confidently. "Death Drop! Leave that poor service worker alone!"

Death Drop's head turned a full 180 degrees to look at Sentry. She bared her razor-sharp teeth at him before laughing sinisterly. She stood, her body turning to match her head. She flexed her fingers. Her razor-sharp nails extended. She pointed at Sentry, and the muscle minions all turned to look at him.

The muscle minions put away their guns. Some put on electrified brass knuckles while others brought out shock batons. Sentry grabbed his discs from his sides. He nearly dropped them when he felt tiny feet rushing up his body. He caught sight of a tiny black mouse that stopped to stand on its hind legs on his shoulder.

"Focus on Death Drop," the mouse squeaked in his ear. "I'll handle the muscle minions."

"Lip-Sync?" Sentry questioned, noticing the red lipstick on the mouse's lips.

Lip-Sync put a clawed finger to her lips. "Sshh. Don't say my name."

"How are you going to take out those muscle minions?" Sentry asked.

Leaping off Sentry's shoulders, Lip-Sync said, "Watch."

Lip-Sync darted around the tables, causing people to shriek in fear. People fell out of their chairs, and tables toppled over as they tried to get away from the furry, four-footed assassin. One of the tables crashed into a muscle minion, knocking him to the ground. A man jumped up from his seat, screaming. He knocked into a muscle minion, and the two fell to the floor, tangled in each other.

Patrons and staff began running from the dashing Lip-Sync in rodent form, knocking the muscle minions about while Death Drop watched in confusion. Sentry took advantage of the distraction and hurled one of his discs at Death Drop.

She turned her head in time for the disc to whack her in the forehead.

Sentry caught the returning disc as Death Drop fell backward, flat on her back. A second later, she popped back up, her eyes blazing with anger. She reached behind her, grabbed the crying waiter by the leg, and hurled him at Sentry.

The waiter flailed in the air, screaming in terror. Sentry ran forward, catching him in his arms. "You're safe now." He set the waiter down on his feet. "Go on, get out of here."

"Thank you," the waiter cried, then rushed past Sentry and out of the door.

Two of the muscle minions started toward Sentry: one with a shock stick and the other with electrified brass knuckles. The one with the electrified brass knuckles paused, and his eyes went wide. He screamed and grabbed his crotch, electrocuting himself in the process. When he fell over, Lip-Sync came running out of his pant leg and up the other.

The other man dropped his shock stick with a yelp. He grabbed his butt and started running around, screaming in pain. He tripped over a fallen chair. Lip-Sync emerged from his pant leg a moment before a group of patrons trampled him as they ran for the exit.

Death Drop stood there, jaw dropped. Sentry threw both of his discs at her—one coming from the right and the other the left. She did a split at the last second, causing the discs to miss. Sentry caught the returning discs. Getting to her feet, Death Drop grabbed the remaining muscle minion and hurled him at Sentry.

Sentry brought his forearms together, raised them, and activated his shields. The muscle minion slammed into the shield. Sentry tossed the man to the side, then lowered his shields. Death Drop let out a hiss. She raised her left hand and formed a gun with her thumb and index finger.

Sentry brought his shields back up, but before Death Drop could let loose her nail barrage, one of the restaurant chandeliers fell on top of her, trapping her underneath. Sentry looked up to see Lip-Sync running up the snapped chain. He looked at the groaning, trapped Death Drop.

"I guess I'm done here." Sentry surveyed the destroyed restaurant.

In front of the fallen demon assassin, a black swirl of smoke appeared. "You may be done, but I'm not." Dante appeared in the smoke.

"What do you want?" Sentry brought his forearms together, raising his shields.

Dante raised his right hand. Red ribbons of magic shot from his fingertips. "Why, you, of course." The magical ribbons avoided Sentry's shields and wrapped around him, binding him. He looked over his shoulder at Death Drop pulling herself from the lighting fixture. "You are worthless."

Death Drop hissed at him. Dante snapped his fingers, and she began sinking into a black pool of magic. "I will deal with you when I get home." Similar black pools of magic appeared around the fallen muscle minions.

"What do you want with me?" Sentry growled, tugging against the magic bonds.

Dante strolled over to Sentry. "I don't want you." He ran a finger under Sentry's chin. "You're the bait for the bear I really want to destroy."

CHAPTER 17

"I DO ENJOY OUR LITTLE WALKS outside," Finn commented as they strolled the perimeter of the laboratory. "I find them quite liberating, don't you?"

Gaymer rubbed the bracelet that ensured his obedience. He couldn't hide the bite in his voice when he spoke. "Very liberating."

"You know, I never really got to look at that magical charm." Finn stopped and took Gaymer's hand. He ran a hand over the bracelet. The bracelet glowed under his touch. "Such an interesting device, isn't it?"

Cautiously, Gaymer said, "Yes. It is."

"Did I tell you how smart I thought you were to sabotage your uncle's weapons when he first used them?" Finn let go of Gaymer's hand and started walking again. "I know Dante ordered you to not do the same to us, but how would we know? We're not programming geniuses like you."

"Right." Gaymer rubbed his wrist. "There is that little deal I struck with you though."

Finn pulled a paper from his inside jacket pocket. "About that. It looks as though that deal is no longer valid. We are unable to fulfill the terms of our deal; therefore, you are released from that obligation." A gust of wind came out of nowhere and took the paper from his hand to land in front of a bush. "Whoops."

"What does that mean?" Gaymer asked.

Finn smiled when, out of the corner of his eye, he saw a tiny black claw snatch the paper and pull it into the bushes. "It means that you should be prepared by midnight tomorrow night."

"Prepared for what? And why midnight tomorrow night?" Gaymer asked, a bit confused.

Finn put an arm around Gaymer. "Because that is when your usefulness will end," he whispered into Gaymer's ear. "Remember the things I told you." He pulled away. "I guess that means you should get back to work."

They both disappeared in a puff of smoke.

"The coms are still down," Salvador announced, a hint of worry in his voice.

Esmeralda ignored him, covertly watching Finn and Gaymer strolling the grounds of the facility with the binoculars. "What are they doing?" she asked before announcing, "He deactivated the bracelet. Why?" She lowered the binoculars. "Where is Freddy? I need to know what was said."

"He and Gato should be making their way back now." Salvador put a hand on her shoulder. "Doesn't it bother you that we can't reach anyone in Morgan City?"

Esmerelda turned to Salvador. "It does, but there is nothing we can do about that here. We have to focus on the mission." She tapped the tablet Salvador had in his other hand. "Did you figure out anything about the ley lines?"

"The only thing I can figure is that we did this. Inadvertently." Salvador held up the pad showing the map. "What I don't get is why DJC Tower is the convergent point."

Esmerelda snapped her fingers. "Because that is where we gather: Sunday brunch, Shadow Command, and any other time we want to train." She thought for a moment. "Don't you feel some strange desire to go there sometimes?"

"I do, and I feel reenergized when I go there." Salvador looked at the pad. "We turned it into a center of magical power for the city."

They turned at the rustling of bushes. Freddy and Gato emerged. "Anything?" Esmerelda asked.

"Yeah, and it's not what we expected," Freddy said, brushing off stray leaves. "He knows we're here, and he sent a very clear message."

Concerned, Esmerelda asked, "What message?"

"See for yourself." Gato handed Esmerelda the note. "He deliberately sent this to land in front of one of my cats spying on him."

Taking the note, Esmerelda read aloud, "Attack at midnight tomorrow when the wards are weakest and the veil between the dimensions are their thinnest."

"The moment when today becomes tomorrow," Salvador said aloud.

Putting an arm around his lover, Freddy added, "It's also a new moon. That means no help from Lunarray if we need it."

"It could be a trap," Gato said, starting to gather up their things. "Why else would he help us?"

Salvador's realization broke their pondering silence. "A power play." They all looked at him. "Demons form alliances all the time to get what they want, then betray the other when it suits them."

"You're saying that the Demon Twinks are working with some unknown demon?" Freddy sniffed the air. "I don't smell another demon."

Esmerelda closed her eyes and cautiously stretched out with her magic. "It makes sense. Those two incubi don't have the power on their own to shield this place." She paused, confusion crossed her face. "There is something ancient and powerful and," Esmerelda opened her eyes, "and cute."

"Shadow Command to anyone who can hear me," Chitter's voice chirped over the coms, "check in, please."

Gato tapped his com. "The Fantastical Four are all accounted for."

"Diego and Alex are never allowed to name our teams ever again," Freddy groaned.

Gato held a finger to his lips. "Shadow Command, what's going on? Why were the coms down?"

"Mamacita, here. Three Peas in a Pod are secure," Juan Carlos's voice cut in. "Why did we let Diego and Alex name these teams?"

Chitter ignored the questions. "Does anyone have eyes on Sentry?"

"Pep Squad here," Dion's voice chimed in. "Seriously, they are not allowed to name teams again. Anyway, I don't have eyes on Sentry but I have eyes on his date. Lip-Sync."

Chitter made a series of worried squeaks. "Does she know what happened to Sentry?"

"Dante the Demon Twink has him," Dion answered solemnly. "She wants to help us get him back."

Esmerelda cut in. "Finn, the other demon twink, sent us a message of when to attack." She exchanged looks with the others. "We're heading back to DJC Tower immediately."

"Same," Juan Carlos added.

There was a series of pops, then Chitter barking. "That's not a good idea. We're still trying to undo the damage Doctor Gingerman and the Three Bears did." They heard Chitter speak to someone off to the side. "Okay, I'll ask." Back on the com, Chitter asked, "Boots is a gargoyle. What does that mean?"

"Gargoyle? I'll ask..." Dion cut herself off. "Okay, Demona says to send Kitty Boy and Boots to In Between immediately. She's opening a portal." Dion paused. "Fantastical Four, you have a stop to make on the way back."

CHAPTER 18

"WHERE IS SHE?" ASPEN SNAPPED as soon as he came through the portal. Following his brother, Aiden ignited his hand. "Yeah, we'll get her to talk."

"Nope." Demona quickly tapped the twins on the forehead with a finger. Aiden's fire extinguished. "This is a neutral, safe space. All are protected here, no matter what."

Aspen glared at Demona. "Fine."

"Where is she?" Aiden asked, his voice not losing his fire. "I want to know what she did with Joshua."

"She's at the bar getting something to eat." Dion stepped forward and took the twins by the hands. "Why don't you two come with me and tell me what happened?"

Keagan, Boots, and Fierce stepped through the portal before it closed. "Diego and Alex are staying behind to try and repair the damage to DJC Tower," Keagan announced, trying to sound tough.

"Look at you two." Demona beamed. "It's not every day that I get to see fated lovers."

Boots and Keagan looked at each other in confusion. "Fated lovers?" they questioned at the same time.

"Meow!" Fierce cried happily.

Demona stepped forward and pulled at an invisible string between the two. "Yes, I am happy they finally realized it too." She let go of the invisible string. "It is forbidden to interfere with the path of fated lovers, to prevent sending them off their path to finding each other."

"I was always meant to be yours." Boots pulled Keagan into his arms.

Keagan ran his hands through Boots' hair. "We were meant for each other."

"Meow," Fierce huffed before walking away.

Keagan yelled after Fierce, "No! We don't need to get a room!"

"That kitten." Demona covered her mouth to hide her laughter. "But if you do need a room, I can arrange that after we talk."

Boots grinned. "Please."

"No!" Keagan blurted, then winked at Boots. "Well, maybe."

"First things first. May I?" Demona pointed to Boots' wings. He nodded. She ran a hand along his wings. "My, my. You have strong, beautiful wings. Thick membranes." She started examining Boots' arm. "Interesting that the rest of you didn't change."

Demona motioned them to a side table. When she saw Boots having a problem sitting, she instructed, "Picture your wings shrinking."

"Okay." Boots closed his eyes and his wings retracted into his body. "It worked!"

Keagan pulled his chair close to Boots. "What does it mean that he's a gargoyle?"

"Gargoyles walk the line of good and evil," Demona explained. "They are wild cards. It is their hearts that determine their allegiance." She nodded to Keagan.

Keagan pointed at himself. "Me?"

Across the room, Fierce crept along the bar toward Lip-Sync eating chicken fingers from a basket. He inched forward, tail in the air. He paused when Ryuu turned and saw him on the bar. He rolled his eyes and returned to setting up his bar, mumbling something under his breath.

Fierce crept closer. He was about to strike and steal a chicken finger when Lip-Sync said, "You know I am a demon assassin, right?"

"Meow!" Fierce cried as he pounced.

Lip-Sync caught the flying kitten by the scruff of his neck. She held Fierce out as he tried to strike her with his claws. Finishing the last piece of chicken, she got up and walked over to the table where Demona, Keagan, and Boots sat. She held Fierce out over the table.

"I believe this belongs to one of you." Lip-Sync dropped Fierce onto the table.

Fierce hissed at Lip-Sync, "Meow!"

"Call me that again, and I'll neuter you," Lip-Sync threatened.

Keagan grabbed Fierce off the table. "You need to learn to be polite."

"Gargoyle, huh?" Lip-Sync eyed Boots. "So that's what Doctor Gingerman was trying to breed in that laboratory."

Demona motioned for Lip-Sync to sit. "Tell us more."

"It couldn't hurt, considering you know most everything anyway." Lip-Sync sat. "Doctor Gingerman has been breeding this special kind of Rage Seed. He had Dante slip the Rage Seed into the Build and Burn chemicals that came from Andrews Inc., but that was a failure. The Rage

Seed never manifested the golems they wanted, just ate away at their souls and drove the people mad because they needed more Build and Burn to survive."

Demona nodded. "The Three Bears."

"The Three Bears," Lip-Sync confirmed. "When I found Teddy, he somehow purged the Rage Seed from his system. I think it was that Drus."

"Jack," Demona added.

Lip-Sync waved her hand. "Whatever his name is. He purged the Rage Seed from Teddy, but when I brought him back to the laboratory, Teddy couldn't be reinfected. His body rejected the Rage Seed. He has a mutated version of the Rage Seed in him that they cannot recreate, so they made a serum using Teddy's blood that stabilized Papa Bear and Honey Bear."

"And Mama Bear," Boots chimed in.

"She was an accident and an anomaly. She was the only test subject that survived, even with the serum," Lip-Sync explained. "Since he couldn't find any living creatures that worked, Doctor Gingerman decided to create one that would. He made them in tubes mixed with both Build and Burn and the serum made from Teddy's blood." She looked over at Boots. "You were the only one to actually make it to term."

Demona asked, "He was an anomaly too, wasn't he?"

"Right. He didn't feel right. Like his existence was an abomination." Lip-Sync smiled at Boots. "Had you not escaped, I was supposed to kill you." She shrugged. "Sorry."

Keagan hissed. "Try it now and see what happens."

"Meow!" Fierce added from the safety of Keagan's lap.

"He'd be dead already if I tried. That's what would happen," Lip-Sync quipped back.

Demona ordered, "Focus!" She pointed a finger at Fierce. "I don't care if you are a guardian. You are still a kitten, so watch your language."

"As I was saying," Lip-Sync continued, unabashed, "they knew the Rage Seed would prevent any magical control, so they had Mayor Trainer test that hypnotic device Doctor Gingerman created that Gaymer improved on."

When Lip-Sync didn't continue, Demona asked, "So what are they up to now?"

"I don't know." Lip-Sync shrugged. "I've been on vacation." She looked at Keagan curiously. "Didn't I hit you with an SUV a few weeks back?"

Boots' body swelled with anger. His voice came out a deep rumbling thunder that shook the bar. "You hurt Keagan!"

"Boots, it's okay. I'm alright," Keagan soothed, taking Boots' hand.

Lip-Sync studied the two curiously. To Demona, she asked, "Fated lovers?"

"Fated lovers," Demona confirmed.

Lip-Sync groaned. "How fairy tale cute."

"Meow!" Fierce retorted.

Lip-Sync put a hand over her chest in mock offense. "The language that kitten uses."

"I'll allow it this time." Demona smiled. "You are being one."

Lip-Sync sighed. "I am, but still, to hear a kitten say it."

"We're working on his language," Keagan said, petting Fierce.

Demona drummed her fingers on the table. "Going after Boots makes sense, but why did they take Joshua? That makes no sense."

"I don't know." Lip-Sync shook her head. "His only connection to all this is," her eyes grew wide, "Teddy and Jack!"

Demona nodded. "He's bait."

"But why?" Lip-Sync questioned. "If the Demon Twinks wanted me to kill him," she motioned over at Boots, "why would they want the means to make more?"

Demona thought for a moment before speaking. "They don't want to make more. They want to prevent more from being made." Demona's voice chilled. "They want to kill Teddy."

"I should get going before the rest of your entourage arrives." Lip-Sync stood. "I'm due back at midnight. I'll do what I can to protect Joshua." Demona created a portal with the twist of her wrist. Lip-Sync gave Keagan and Boots a pained smile. "Fated lovers. It's good to see that love is still out there for some." Then she stepped through.

CHAPTER 19

"WHY DID YOU LET HER GO?" Aiden and Aspen shrieked, rushing up to Demona.

Herc appeared behind them. Lifting the twins by the back of the pants, he admonished, "Mind your manners or I'll throw you out."

"It's okay, Herc." Demona motioned for him to put them down. "Put them down."

Strolling in, Juan Carlos scolded, "It is not okay. My children should know better." He took Demona's hand and kissed it with a flourish. "I apologize for their rude behavior."

"Wait," Aspen said, still dangling from Herc's fist. "When did we become his children?"

"The moment he decided he liked you," Dion answered, coming up and hugging Juan Carlos.

"It's so good to see you're safe. Where are Aaron and Felipe?"

Juan Carlos returned the hug. "Dealing with that restaurant mess." He smiled at Keagan and Boots. "I'm glad to see the new members of our family are safe."

"I'm a gargoyle, and we're fated lovers," Boots boasted proudly, putting an arm around Keagan. "We get to touch each other in our underwear areas!"

Keagan's cheeks flushed red and his eyes went wide with embarrassment. "Can we forget he said that last part?" he pleaded. "Please?"

"Nope," Aiden answered, still dangling in Herc's grasp.

Demona shook her head, stifling a laugh. "Not a chance."

"Be nice, everyone," Juan Carlos playfully scolded. "He's new."

Aspen tapped Herc on the chest. "Excuse me, but could you put us down now?"

"Behave," Herc ordered, dropping them to their feet, "or else."

Aspen straightened his clothes. "Now maybe we can have our powers back? We have a demon assassin to track down."

"Sit. Listen." Demona snapped her fingers. Chairs popped up under Aiden and Aspen. "You can have your powers back when you show you can use them responsibly."

Aiden raised his hand. "Um, when you give us back our powers, do you think Herc would swirl me around as Fire? It would look so cool."

"How are we even related?" Aspen groaned.

Aiden pointed at himself then Aspen. "Duh, we're twins."

"I really must start limiting his exposure to Diego." Juan Carlos sighed, taking Lip-Sync's vacated seat.

Pulling up a chair, Dion asked, "Does it worry anyone besides me that his answer made perfect sense?"

"It worries me immensely. What worries me more is this coordinated attack. Why did they take Joshua?" Juan Carlos asked, a bit troubled.

Coldly, Aspen said, "Ask Demona. She's the one that let Lip-Sync go."

"This is a neutral space. She couldn't hold Lip-Sync here if she wanted," Juan Carlos defended.

Demona smiled at Juan Carlos. "Thank you, but my conversation with Lip-Sync was very enlightening. Here, allow me." She tapped everyone around the table on the forehead, sharing her memory of the conversation with Lip-Sync.

"Fierce!" Juan Carlos snatched the kitten from Keagan's lap by the scruff of the neck. "Listen here.

I don't care that you're some big, bad guardian. You are still a kitten. If I ever hear you use that type of language again, you and I are going to have a problem."

Fierce let out an apologetic "Meow."

"That's better." Juan Carlos cuddled Fierce. "I hate disciplining my grandchildren."

Boots looked over at Keagan. "Juan Carlos is your father?"

"No," Keagan groaned. "We got adopted."

Smiling as warmly as he could, Aspen said, "Welcome to the family."

"Do we know when the others can get here?" Juan Carlos asked, Fierce purring against his chest.

Dion pulled out her phone. "The Fantastical Four won't be back until after midnight. Alex sent an update. They don't know when they'll be able to undo whatever Doctor Gingerman did to the building."

Chitter barked and squeaked angrily. Alegro vibrated their frustration as well as they attempted to regain some control of the building. To Chitter's left, Diego worked diligently to decipher the code that held the building hostage while Alex did the same on Alegro's right.

"I can't make heads nor tails of this code," Diego growled.

Alex shook his head. "It's as confusing as that hypnotic code Juan Carlos had me trying to break."

"Wait." Chitter popped their head up. They twitched their whiskers. "The hypnotic code."

Alex slammed his hand on the console. "All the code is in my lab at DJC Headquarters."

"I have the code." Chitter flipped their tail back and forth. "Now that I know his style." Chitter's black eyes flashed as he transferred the code to Alegro. "We can break his control on the building."

Diego patted the top of Chitter's head. "When this is all over, I want you to give us a crash course in his code."

"Roger that," Chitter barked with a salute.

Alex stroked Alegro. "You two did good out there. I'm proud of both of you."

"Those acorn bombs worked great." Diego smiled proudly. "That was a great idea you two had."

Alex quickly added, "Don't think this means you get to come into battle with us."

Alegro vibrated under Alex's touch.

"Alegro's right," Chitter chirped defiantly. "You're going to need us out there, and you're not leaving me behind when we go rescue Gaymer." Chitter crossed their tiny arms. "Besides, Diego already said we could."

Alex glared at his boyfriend. "What?"

"The treehouse is really a Mobile Shadow Command Center," Diego answered guiltily. "Chitter and Alegro designed it while we were on vacation. I helped them with design aspects and some additions this morning."

Alex scooped up Alegro into his arms. "My baby is not going into battle!" He snatched up Chitter. "Or my..." Perplexed, he looked at Chitter. "Squirrel friend?"

"Squirrel friend," Chitter confirmed.

Alex returned to glaring at Diego. "Or my squirrel friend!"

"Mobile Shadow Command is only going to be used when we need it, like controlling Shadow Drone squadrons or the scurry of squirrel drones."

Alex blinked. "The scurry of what?" Alegro zipped over to Diego, and Chitter leaped from Alex to land on Diego's shoulder. Alex crossed his arms. "Answers. Now."

"It was all Chitter's idea!" Diego grabbed the squirrel and held them out to Alex.

Wriggling in Diego's outstretched hands, Chitter barked, "I'm no longer your squirrel friend, traitor!"

"Answers," Alex demanded, taking Chitter from Diego. "Now."

Chitter shot a dirty look at a remorseful Diego before looking at Alex with as much sweetness and innocence as they could muster. "We haven't made any yet, but imagine Shadow Guardian leading hundreds of drone squirrels into battle."

Alex began laughing. "I can, and it's the laugh I needed tonight." He set Chitter down on the console.

"At least they wouldn't look like go-go boys in battle," Chitter barked angrily.

Diego recoiled at Alex's scathing look. "About that," his lips curled into a smile, "we're going to keep that look for a while."

"Really?" Diego brightened. "What about my robotic squirrel army?"

Alex patted the top of Chitter's head. "Don't push your luck. The last thing anyone wants to hear is you commanding them to 'nut all over' someone."

"That was bad, wasn't it?" Diego chuckled. "The look on Papa Bear's face."

Alegro vibrated around Diego.

"Alegro thinks he broke Doctor Gingerman's code!" Chitter shouted merrily. "He's purging Doctor Gingerman's code from the building's systems now!"

Diego snuggled his shapeless child. "Good work."

"Now, about our Mobile Shadow Command Center." Rubbing their front paws together, Chitter looked at Alex imploringly.

Alex crossed his arms. "As long as you stay safe and away from any fighting." He pointed a finger at Chitter. "And no drone squirrel army." He turned to Diego. "I mean it."

"Okay, I promise." Diego held up his hands. "I promise."

Chitter flipped their tail back and forth. "Fine. No drone squirrel army."

"I mean it." Alex darted his eyes from Diego to Chitter.

Diego pulled Alex into a hug. "I heard you."

"Right," Chitter chirped merrily. "No squirrel army."

CHAPTER 20

STRIPPED DOWN TO HIS SOCKS AND yellow happy face boxer briefs, Joshua sat slumped on the cot in his cell. He ran his thumb over the medallion Teddy and Jack gave him.

His stomach grumbled. He wondered if they'd feed him, not that he'd trust anything they gave him. He would have to wait until he was rescued to eat, but how would they find him? Did anyone know he was gone? The coms were down when the Demon Twink took him.

Lip-Sync, Joshua thought. *She'll get word to my friends, somehow.*

Joshua looked up when the doors slid open. Lip-Sync strolled in carrying a basket of chicken fingers. "I brought you something to eat." She held the basket through the bars. "From In Between."

"Thank you." Joshua scrambled off the cot to take the basket. Wolfing down fries, he said, "I'm starving."

Lip-Sync lowered her gaze down to Joshua's boxers. Judgmentally, she pointed at his crotch. "You wore those on our date?"

"What?" Joshua asked, biting down on a piece of chicken. "They're cute."

She tapped her finger in thought on her cheek. "I sort of figured you for a thong guy."

"No, you didn't." Joshua shoved fries into his mouth.

Lip-Sync rolled her eyes. "Your table manners are atrocious."

"We're not at a table." Joshua wiped his mouth with the back of his hand. "Did you bring me anything to drink?"

Lip-Sync held up her hand. A cup appeared. "Chocolate strawberry oat milk shake." She handed it over. "Would you like a cake with a file baked in it too?" She held up her other hand. A slab of chocolate cake with red icing appeared. "Here."

"Thank you." Joshua juggled the food.

Cryptically, Lip-Sync said, "Make sure you savor every bite of that cake. I baked it especially for you." Her eyes caught the glitter of gold on Joshua's chest. She grabbed the medallion through the bars. Curious, she asked, "Where did you get this from?"

"Jack and Teddy gave it to me before I left the forest." Joshua pulled away, pulling the medallion from her grasp. Setting the food aside, he suspiciously asked, "Why?"

Shaking her head, Lip-Sync lied, "No reason." Before he could call her out on the lie, Lip-Sync shared, "Don't try to escape. It's not safe out there. You're not in the laboratory where Gaymer is. Dante put you in a pocket dimension that I didn't even know existed before now."

"What do you expect me to do?" Joshua growled.

Lip-Sync winked. "You have my cake. Why don't you eat it too." She turned and started to leave. Over her shoulder, she said, "Take care of that necklace."

"Take care of the necklace?" Joshua held up the medallion around his neck. "Okay." He shrugged before returning to his meal.

"Where is everyone?" Esmerelda asked, strolling into In Between.

Demona yawned. "If you mean the patrons, you tell me. We haven't had a customer all night. If you mean everyone else, well, since DJC Tower is locked down thanks to Doctor Gingerman, Juan Carlos is spending the night with Dion. Aiden and Aspen are spending the night with Boots and Keagan."

"What happened?" Salvador asked, giving Demona a hug.

Demona tapped Salvador on the forehead, sharing her knowledge. "Much easier." She did the same for Freddy, Esmeralda, and Gato.

"Turnabout is fair play." Esmerelda shared her knowledge with Demona.

Demona raised an eyebrow. "Why would he do that?"

"Something doesn't feel right about all this," Freddy growled. "First they take Gaymer, and now they want to conveniently give him back. Why?"

Gato took a seat at the bar. He motioned to Ryuu for a drink. "At least now we know why they took Joshua. Too bad Jack and Teddy can't help."

"His forest is packed full of mystical creatures." Esmerelda took a seat beside Gato. "He can't leave it or the mysticals there unprotected, and Teddy is still too weak to do anything."

Salvador went behind the bar and began making him and Freddy a drink. "If they are trying to lure Teddy and Jack out, why would they tell us when their defenses are their weakest?"

"Ours will be as well," Freddy commented, taking the glass filled with sparkling blue liquid from his boyfriend. Smiling, he said, "A Midsummer's Night." He tapped the side of the highball glass. Tiny sparks of light flashed in the glass.

Ryuu sat a pink squirrel in front of Esmerelda. "Except you now have a gargoyle on your side."

"That is true." Esmerelda eyed the drink with black licorice wrapped around the stem. "I didn't order this."

Demona laughed softly. "That's his way of saying he misses Chitter and Alegro."

"Andrea and I enjoy playing hide-and-seek with them in the forest." Ryuu smiled. "They also know how to get at those hard to reach itches under my scales."

Freddy brightened. "Hide-and-seek? Can I play?"

"Of course." Ryuu smiled. "The more the merrier."

Esmerelda looked at a fidgeting Gato and shook her head. "You can play too if you want."

"It's going to be so much fun!" Gato proclaimed.

Demona tapped the bar. "Can we focus back on the dilemma at hand?"

"There is something we're missing, a piece of the puzzle." Esmeralda sipped the cocktail. "I like this."

Ryuu smiled. "Thank you."

"Could it be Boots?" Freddy asked, tapping his drink again. "He's still an unknown."

Demona bit her lip in thought. "Maybe. He emerged as a gargoyle. Sort of." Demona tapped the bar with a finger. "He seems to be the source of conflict between the Demon Twinks and Doctor Gingerman."

"The note from Madam Zelda warned of a coming war," Gato commented. "Could this be it?"

Demona nodded her head. "My mothers warned me of the same thing."

"We should prepare for the fallout," Ryuu nodded. "There's going to be a huge influx of refugees on both sides."

Demona shook her head. "With the ley lines realigned, we are going to be limited on how many we can house."

"How did that happen without us noticing?" Esmeralda asked, stirring her drink.

Demona threw up her hands. "We're all still frequenting the same places, plus the distractions. Who knows what else we have missed?"

"Then we attack tomorrow at midnight?" Freddy asked before finally downing his drink. He burped tiny sparkles. "Excuse me."

Gato sighed. "It doesn't look like we have much of a choice, does it? We gather the troops and rescue our friends."

Dante glared over at Doctor Gingerman and his scratched up face. Two of his laboratory technicians were at his side, cleaning up the scratches. With a wave of his hand, he could heal the man, but Dante refused to offer. He deserved this reminder of his failure.

"Let me understand this," Dante said venomously. "You not only failed to get Experiment B12, but you were also bested by a kitten?"

Doctor Gingerman motioned his technicians away. They collected the medical supplies then quickly left. "He was more than a kitten," Doctor Gingerman spat out. "We also weren't expecting that pink fur ball or those blasted twins to be there."

"You should have." Dante crossed his arms. "I was prepared in case one of the other heroes showed up."

Doctor Gingerman picked up his white dog and sat it in his lap. Calmly petting it, he asked, "About that, where is our prize? He's not here."

"I put him somewhere safe. I thought it prudent to keep our prisoners in different locations." He emphasized his next words. "Being that it was I that secured them both," Dante smiled sinisterly, "I didn't think you would object."

Doctor Gingerman's dog growled. He calmed it with a stroke along its back. "You'll bring him here as planned, or else."

"I won't be doing that." Dante examined his nails. "This partnership has been completely one-sided lately." He glared at Doctor Gingerman. "Start pulling your weight."

Doctor Gingerman gritted his teeth. "Don't forget who summoned you out of that Hell dimension and guided you to secure more power. None of this would be possible if it wasn't for our planning and our sacrifices."

"Yes, daddy, I remember." Dante's eyes flared red. "I also remember you risking my wellbeing to secure you those blasted Rage Seeds that turned out to be a complete failure."

Doctor Gingerman stood. Setting the dog down in the chair, he turned to face Dante. "Listen here, you little brat." The building shook and the lights flickered. "You will do as you are told or you will suffer the consequences."

"What? Are you going to spank me?" Dante asked flippantly. "You have no power over me." Dante waved a hand. The dog let out a yelp when the chair she was sitting on started slowly sucking her in. "I know your weakness."

Doctor Gingerman dashed to the dog and tried to pull her free. "Dante!" he bellowed. "Stop this now!"

"Remember that." Dante released the dog with another wave of his hand.

Holding the dog to his chest, Doctor Gingerman turned to face Dante. "Oh, I'll remember."

"I'm glad we have an understanding." Dante yawned. "I'm going to get some rest. Have a good night." With that, he vanished with a puff of smoke.

Doctor Gingerman cradled the dog to his chest. "It is time we rid ourselves of those annoying Demon Twinks."

CHAPTER 21

DOCTOR TYSON LOOKED UP FROM his console to check on Chitter and Alegro. They were unusually quiet at their work station. "What are you two up to?"

"Nothing," Chitter answered, looking back at him before returning their attention to their work.

Doctor Tyson rubbed his temples. "Alex said not to let you create a drone squirrel army."

"We're not making an army," Chitter retorted. Alegro vibrated and Chitter relented. Turning to face Doctor Tyson, Chitter explained, "We're making specialized Shadow Drones for the attack tonight."

Curiosity got the better of Doctor Tyson. "Let me see." He studied the screen. "Interesting. Do you mind if I suggest some design changes?"

Alegro vibrated.

"Thank you." Doctor Tyson began typing on the screen. "If we use natural design elements, we can increase their efficiency and maneuverability."

Alegro vibrated.

"Yes, they'll be scarier too." Doctor Tyson laughed. "They'll also be able to hold more types of ammunition."

Alegro vibrated.

"Hhmm, yes, we could change the impact acorns to deliver different types of attacks." Doctor Tyson brought up the acorn schematics. "We can adapt what we have from Shadow Guardian and High Tech."

Chitter looked at Alegro then at Doctor Tyson. "You can understand Alegro?"

"Huh?" Doctor Tyson thought for a moment. "I can. Alex said he was uploading a patch into the communication network. It must have installed a translation program for Alegro."

Alegro vibrated excitedly.

"Yes, it is great to be able to talk to you directly." Doctor Tyson smiled.

Chitter whipped their tail back and forth excitedly. "This means when I go home with Gaymer, you'll still be able to talk to everyone."

Alegro vibrated softly.

"Well, I guess I'll be leaving when we get Gaymer back. I don't know where we'd go, though." Chitter hugged Alegro. "We're still going to be best squirrel friends."

Alegro wrapped around Chitter. They vibrated softly.

"Exactly, Alegro. You'll still see each other at work and when Gaymer comes to visit Aspen." Doctor Tyson smiled again.

Alegro vibrated around Chitter then pulled away.

"Right! Let's get back to work!" Chitter brushed themself off. "We need to pull our weight to get Gaymer and Joshua back."

Doctor Tyson typed on the console. "What do you two think of this for your Mobile Shadow Command Center?"

Alegro vibrated excitedly.

"I love it too!" Chitter jumped up and down excitedly.

Boots zoomed through the room, dodging Fire's blasts. Below, Kitty Boy leapt about the obstacle course, dodging Ice's attacks. Fierce was at the tiny control console gleefully hitting buttons randomly that activated obstacles and traps. Kitty Boy jumped up, and Boots grabbed his hands.

Boots flung him at Fire. Hitting her in the chest, he then kicked off to tackle Ice.

"No you don't, Kitty." Ice quickly created a snow drift that Kitty Boy found himself stuck in headfirst. "Or you." Ice quickly stepped aside as Boots came diving down at her, only to find himself crashing to the other side of the snow mound. "Okay, brush yourselves off. We will go again in five minutes."

Fire melted the snow mound with a touch. "No, we're done for now." She helped Kitty Boy up. "We've been running drills all day." She did the same to Boots then hit them with a blast of hot air to dry them. "We need to rest and recharge."

"When we're in battle, we're not going to get to rest and recharge." Ice stomped her high-heeled foot on the ground, causing the ground to freeze underneath. "We go again in five minutes."

Kitty Boy stretched. "Fire is right. We need more than five minutes, and Fierce needs to use the litter box."

"Meow!" Fierce called out, scratching at the door.

Boots shuffled uncomfortably. "I could use the litter box too."

"Go." Ice pointed to the door.

Boots rushed off. Fire tapped Kitty Boy's shoulder. "He's not really going to use a litter box, is he?"

"No." Kitty Boy thought for a moment. "I'll be right back."

Ice shook her head. "We're never going to be ready."

"We'll get Gaymer and Joshua back." Fire pulled her sister into a hug. "We're more than ready."

Ice returned the hug. "How can you be sure? We couldn't defeat the Demon Twink, and we were nearly defeated by the Pups."

"The Demon Twink used Gaymer against you; otherwise, you would have kicked his skinny butt." Fire brushed a frozen tear from Ice's cheek. "The Pups, well, they had numbers."

Ice transformed back into Aspen. "What do you think they'll have when we attack?"

"More than they can handle." Fire turned back into Aiden. "This time we have Esmerelda, Gato, Freddy, Salvador, Keagan, and Boots."

Aspen pulled away. "Is it going to be enough, though?"

"It will be." There was a bit of humor in Aiden's voice when he said, "If not, we have our mischievous trio."

Aspen fought the smile that spread across his lips. "They did pretty well last night. I'm betting

Chitter and Alegro are coming up with some outlandish idea that is going to save the day."

"Meow," Fierce said, trotting in.

Aspen looked at the kitten. "What do you mean it's not an outlandish plan?"

"Meow," Fierce answered, sitting down and starting to groom himself.

Aiden looked at the kitten suspiciously. "'You'll see' is not an answer. What do you know?"

"Meow," Fierce responded smugly.

Aiden cocked an eyebrow. "Ask my boyfriend?"

"I wasn't going to use the litter box," Boots grumbled at Kitty Boy.

Kitty Boy grumbled back, "I had to make sure."

"They're cute." Aspen smiled, putting hand over his heart.

"We're more than cute." Boots scooped Kitty Boy up in his arms. With a flap of his mighty wings, they rose in the air. "We're fated lovers."

Kitty Boy quickly wrapped his arm around Boots' neck. "I wish you would stop telling people that."

"No telling people we're fated lovers." Boots flew up higher into the air. "No telling people we get to touch each other in our underwear places." Boots did a quick loop. "What *can* I tell people?"

Kitty Boy clung closer. "That you love your boyfriend."

206

"Boyfriend." Boots stopped and hovered in the air. He smiled at Kitty Boy. He flew around the room doing spirals and loops, yelling, "He called me his boyfriend!"

Aiden rested an elbow on Aspen's shoulder. "They are cute."

"Why exactly did you let Joshua go out on a date with Lip-Sync?" Aspen asked, changing the subject.

Aiden sighed. "Call me a hopeless romantic, but I thought enemies to lovers, forbidden love, second chances, and stuff like that."

"You really need to stop reading so many romantic novels." Aspen chuckled, watching Boots land carefully in front of them. "On second thought, I think we do have a chance." He smiled. "We have love on our side."

Boots sat Kitty Boy down. "Shall we go again?"

"No." Aspen surprised everyone with his answer. "We're going up to our apartment to relax. We've earned it."

Gato busied himself in the kitchen while Esmerelda sat on her sofa drinking her tea. Beside her sat Salvador, quietly sipping his tea. The silence in the room was only broken by Freddy curled up on the loveseat softly snoring. Salvador hummed a soft tune. Purple wisps of magic flowed from his song to silence Freddy's snoring.

"I remember when he couldn't sleep the day of the new moon," Esmerelda mused. "How things have changed."

Salvador let out a snort of laughter. "You mean before I found out you turned me into a siren mutation and I had to get a crash course on magic?"

"Technically, I didn't turn you into a siren mutation. One of my previous lives did." Esmerelda set her cup on the coffee table. "It's hard to believe we are still fighting the same enemy from back then, sort of."

Salvador finished his tea, then put his cup down. "Something seems strange about it, you know?"

"Yes," Esmerelda shifted on the couch, "like this is another domino falling."

Salvador looked at his boyfriend. "But which way does the domino fall?"

"Wherever Madam Zelda decided it should," Gato answered, bringing in a tray of meats and cheeses. "How she has been guiding all of this, I don't know."

Esmeralda took a piece of cheese from the plate. "She ascended. She's probably annoying

Fate and Destiny with her actions." Esmerelda laughed. "She really has a twisted sense of humor making Keagan a champion and Boots a gargoyle." She made a face. "Sort of."

"He's not really a gargoyle, is he?" Gato asked, taking a seat beside her. "He has wings, but his body is human."

Esmerelda patted Gato on his knee. "Gargoyles are rare. Most were killed in the battles of the Heavens and Hells. Those that are left do not associate with any mysticals because they were betrayed by both sides."

"Boots has an innocence that is so endearing." Salvador smiled. "When I went and got him from their apartment, he hugged me and told me he was a gargoyle. That he had wings and could fly."

Freddy yawned and stretched. He sniffed the air. "Food." He grabbed a few pieces of meat from the plate. "Are we talking about the other fated lovers?" he asked around a mouthful of food. "Because the way Boots gets Keagan all flustered and makes his cheeks flush red is hilarious."

"Their bond is really strong, as strong as yours and Salvador's." Esmerelda thought for a moment. "You know, we should take a look at Alex and Diego's bond."

Gato nodded. "Agreed."

"Let's just not look too closely at their bond."
Salvador smirked. "They are an odd couple."

"It's done," Alex announced, stretching out on
the couch. Diego handed him his coffee. "You are
the best."

Diego kissed Alex on the forehead. "One less
thing to worry about." He took a seat on the couch.
He watched the wall slowly repairing itself. "It's
nice to have a self-repairing building."

"We might want to think about installing emer-
gency exits in Shadow Command." Alex took a
healthy sip of his coffee. "That is so good."

Diego put an arm around Alex. "Already in the
works. The new couch is on the way, and Doctor
Tyson messaged that he upgraded the Mobile
Shadow Command Center to include the shield
tech you and Sentry use." He kissed Alex on the
cheek. "He said your patch went through and it
works. He can understand Alegro now."

"That's great!" Alex couldn't help the grin that
spread across his face. "I know they don't act like
it, but I know Alegro felt like an outsider not being
able to talk to us directly."

Diego hugged Alex, nearly making him spill
his coffee. "You're such a great dad."

"And you're a naughty papi," Alex teased. "Seriously? An army of drone squirrels?"

Diego laughed. "I thought it was a great idea when Chitter pitched it."

"From now on, all new ideas get approval from me." Alex snuggled against Diego.

Diego smiled impishly. "All new ideas?"

"Yes, and," Alex took another long, healthy sip of his coffee, "before you ask, no. I'm tired."

Diego sulked. "Fine."

"Ask me again after we rescue our friends." Alex patted him on the chest. "I won't be as grumpy then."

Diego grew serious. "About tonight, are you up for it?"

"Last night, I didn't think. I needed to protect my friends, my child, and you." Alex's voice went distant. "I didn't think I was capable of that, but I did it." He smiled at Diego. "I'm not only ready for tonight. I'm up for it."

Diego kissed Alex. "I want you to be careful tonight. Don't take any unnecessary risks." He hugged Alex tighter. "After this, I want to take you to meet my parents."

"Your parents?" Alex shot up. "You know where they are?" Diego nodded. "Wow, I'm glad you found them and made up with them. What made you look for them? Does Juan Carlos know?"

211

Diego's smile faltered a bit. "It was Felipe finding Juan Carlos that made me want to find my parents. I haven't told Juan Carlos yet that I found them." He ran a finger over Alex's cheek. "I was waiting for the right moment to tell him."

"I can't wait to meet them," Alex said excitedly.

Diego pulled himself away and stood. "We should get ready. Everyone will be here soon."

CHAPTER 22

"THE DEMON TWINKS HAVE OUT-lived their usefulness," Doctor Gingerman announced to the Three Bears as he paced the room. "We will be moving our operations to Morgan City."

Mama Bear growled. "It's about time. Their very existence is an affront to my delicate nature."

"Your nature is anything but delicate," Papa Bear scoffed.

Mama Bear touched the bracelet on her arm. Papa Bear jerked about in pain before falling onto the floor. "Mind your manners, Papa."

"We'll be doing a scorched earth." Doctor Gingerman nudged the groaning Papa Bear with his foot. "Get up, you worthless bag of flesh."

Papa Bear groaned. Pulling himself up from the floor, he growled angrily. "Yes, Doctor

Gingerman." Sitting back down beside Mama Bear, he mumbled under his breath, "I'll have my revenge on all of them."

"What was that?" Mama Bear asked, finger poised over her bracelet.

Seeing the threat, Papa Bear said through gritted teeth, "I'm sorry, Doctor Gingerman. I'll do better."

"I thought so." She patted Papa Bear on the leg. "Good boy."

Doctor Gingerman glared at Papa Bear. "As I was saying, scorched earth. You three will be responsible for getting Gaymer and his research."

"What about the Demon Twinks?" Honey Bear asked, giggling madly. "They aren't going to let us take Gaymer and the research."

Doctor Gingerman picked up his white lapdog. "Leave that up to us." He petted the growling dog. "We strike at midnight when today becomes tomorrow. You'll have one minute to get in and get out before the pocket dimension phases out of this one. Five minutes after that, the bombs will go off, turning this facility into a pile of rubble."

"Explosions!" Honey Bear exclaimed with glee. "I like it when things go boom!"

Mama Bear patted him on the head. "I know you do, dear." She turned her attention to Doctor Gingerman. "How are you going to plant the explosives without those filthy twinks finding out?"

"With our new recruit." Doctor Gingerman opened a side door. Stepping aside, Death Drop stepped through. "We're not the only ones who detest those twinks." Exposing her razor-sharp teeth with a smile, Death Drop waved with a wiggle of her fingers. "She's placed explosives throughout the laboratory. The three of you are to complete your mission then meet me here."

Papa Bear snarled, "What is she going to be doing?"

"Retrieving the rest of our property." Doctor Gingerman put a hand on her shoulder.

Honey Bear vibrated in his seat. "Can we keep one of them for me to play with?"

"No, sweetie." Mama Bear patted him on the head. "They are filthy, disgusting creatures. How about we get you that Kitty Boy to play with instead? After we declaw him, of course."

Honey Bear bounced in his seat. "Can I have that go-go boy too?"

"Hhmm, if you're a good Honey Bear." Mama Bear gave a saccharine smile.

Papa Bear groaned. "He's just going to tear them apart, and we'll have pink fur and body glitter all over the place."

Mama Bear put an arm around Papa Bear. "Did you want the go-go boy for yourself?"

"No," Papa Bear snarled, "I want Diego Sanz's head mounted on my wall."

Mama Bear thought for a moment. "I think I know the best place to hang it."

"If you three are done playing house," Doctor Gingerman cut in angrily, "we have plans to set in motion." He sneered at Papa Bear. "Oh, and try not to be bested by squirrels."

Papa Bear muttered, "Big talk coming from a man who was taken down by a kitten."

"That was no mere kitten!" Doctor Gingerman's thunderous voice silenced their snickering. "I will have that creature's hide decorating my penthouse! Now go! And don't fail me if you value your own skin!"

The Three Bears rushed out of the room past Death Drop and Doctor Gingerman. Death Drop faced Doctor Gingerman. Saluting him, she marched out, comically swinging the opposite arm to the leg she kicked up. Shutting the door behind her, Doctor Gingerman let out a sigh.

"Good help is so hard to find." Doctor Gingerman petted the white dog in his arm. "Soon, we'll be done with all of them, and our plans will come to fruition." He set the dog down in his chair. "Every realm and every dimension will bow down before us."

CHAPTER 23

"**I** SAW DEATH DROP SNEAKING OUT of Doctor Gingerman's office," Finn commented, straightening Dante's tie. "We can assume she's compromised."

Dante pecked him on the cheek. "That was expected. That foul creature doesn't know the meaning of loyalty."

"What about Lip-Sync?" Finn asked, brushing the lapels of Dante's jacket. "Can we trust her?"

Dante turned to inspect himself in the mirror. "Trust her? Yes. Rely upon her? No." He turned and wrapped Finn in his arms. "She has been distracted by her heart."

"What about you?" Finn put his hands on Dante's hips. "Have you been distracted by your heart?"

Dante grinned. "My heart has shown me the way to true power." He kissed Finn lightly. "Have all the pieces been put into play?"

"If the whispers are to be believed." Finn pulled away. From their desk, he snatched a flash drive. Holding it up, he said, "This will get my point across in case my hints weren't obvious enough."

Dante put his arm around Finn's waist. "Then shall we pay our dear Gaymer visit?"

There. A default ten second command life is hidden perfectly in his code. Gaymer smiled proudly. *With three auto factory reset triggers if anyone tries to alter it.*

Gaymer turned at the smell of brimstone. "Can't you guys do something about that smell?" Gaymer asked, waving his hand in front of his face.

"Next time, I will make it smell like cotton candy, candy canes, and unicorns," Dante responded sarcastically.

Gaymer returned the comment with an equally sarcastic, "Could you? That would be simply splendid."

"Enough pleasantries." Dante cut his eyes at Finn when he heard him snickering. "How is our little project going? No sabotages, correct?"

Dante grinned. "I would really hate for this plan of Doctor Gingerman's to fail like all his other plans."

Finn stepped into action, taking Gaymer's hand and slipping him the flash drive. "Of course not. Gaymer and I have made strides in our relationship. He would never put anything in the computers that I did not give him."

"Right." Gaymer palmed the drive, then stuck his hands into his pants pockets. "I would never do anything to sabotage the project given everything that is at stake."

Finn smiled at Dante. "See, I told you that I could get him to cooperate, and he'll meet our midnight deadline."

"Midnight." Gaymer nodded. "Everything will be ready at midnight."

Dante sighed. "If only everything was this simple."

"I'll be back at midnight." Finn winked at Gaymer before going to stand beside Dante. "We better get going. We have dinner reservations."

Dante slipped an arm around Finn. "Shall we?"

Joshua sat in his cell, twirling the flash drive Lip-Sync had hidden in the slice of cake. *What good is this for me in here?* He looked up to see the

Demon Twinks enter. Slipping the drive into his underwear, he stood. "What do you two want?"

"Rude." Finn clacked his tongue. "Can we not pay our favorite prisoner a visit?"

Dante eyed him. "Favorite prisoner? He's not even my favorite hero to battle."

"He's sort of adorable." Finn grinned. "Can we keep him as a pet?"

"I'm nobody's pet!" Joshua snapped.

"No." Dante sighed. "You say you'll walk him, feed him, and bathe him, but whose muscle minions will end up doing it?"

Joshua crossed his arms over his chest, hiding his gold medallion. He repeated, "What do you want?"

"Honestly, we were bored and wanted to play with you." Dante grinned threateningly. "How loud can you scream?"

Finn laughed. "Quit teasing him."

"Oh, you're no fun." Dante took Finn by the hand and twirled him. "I wanted to see how he'd react." He dipped Finn.

Popping back up, Finn put his arms around Dante's waist. "Oh, my love, we don't have time for games." Finn pulled away to face Joshua. "We were in the neighborhood feasting and thought we'd drop in and see how you're doing." Finn glanced at Joshua's happy face boxer briefs. "Who dresses you?"

"I wasn't expected to be kidnapped, stripped, and tossed in a cell," Joshua huffed angrily.

Dante put an arm over Finn's shoulders. "You should always dress to be undressed."

"Are you sure we can't keep him as a pet? He's already housebroken." Finn grinned. "We could dress him in cute little outfits and post the pictures on social media!"

Dante tousled Finn's brown hair. "No."

"You two are annoying." Joshua returned to his cot. "I hope my friends rescue me soon."

Finn let out a bark of laughter. "They aren't going to rescue you."

"You are in a Hell dimension that only a few even remember." Dante chortled. "No one is coming to rescue you."

Joshua stared at them coldly. "We'll see."

CHAPTER 24

"**I**'M NOT SAYING THEY ARE A BAD driver," Alex argued, stepping out of the back of the converted 22-foot box truck. "What I'm saying is that I don't think you should have had Chitter drive us here."

Following behind him, Diego countered, "Why? Sure, they flipped off one car that cut them off, but they obeyed all the traffic laws and got us here safely."

"Help me here," Alex pleaded with Salvador as he stepped down.

Salvador gave him a sympathetic look. "Diego has a point, and he looked really cute in that tiny jean vest and ballcap."

"Don't look at me." Freddy grinned at Alex. "I want him to be on my team in hide-and-seek."

Gato followed behind Freddy. He extended a hand to help Esmerelda down. "There aren't any teams in hide-and-seek."

"You haven't played with them." Esmerelda took Gato's hands. "They have unusual rules."

Alex groaned when he saw Diego's eyes light up. "You can play too if you want." He winked at Diego. "As long as I get to play too."

"I'm guessing we'll be patrolling those nights." Aspen gingerly stepped down.

Boots jumped down from the truck. "Can I play too?"

"Only if you take me and Fierce with you." Keagan appeared in the doorway holding Fierce.

Fierce jumped from Keagan's arms as he stepped down. Boots caught him and snuggled him. "Meow!"

"So who is going to unload this thing?" Aiden asked, pointing behind him as he exited. "Unloading a truck of Shadow Drones is not in my job description."

The passenger side window lowered. Chitter, wearing their tiny ballcap and jean vest, poked their head out the window. "I'll deploy them as needed." The top of the truck opened, and the circular Mobile Shadow Command Center rose from it. It zoomed down to the window. "Looks like my new ride is ready." Chitter ducked down only to reappear wearing goggles similar to Gaymer's on his head and a red-blue jacket. "Let's get squirrely."

"No, that's not going to be a thing," Alex said, shaking his head. Chitter and Alegro jumped from the truck to the Mobile Shadow Command Center. "You two be careful."

Alegro vibrated.

"I'm your dad. I reserve the right to be worried," Alex countered, crossing his arms. "For you and our squirrel friend."

Diego put a hand on Alex's shoulder. "They'll be fine. They have the shield technology in the Mobile Shadow Command Center." He looked to the rest. "Shall we go over the plan again?"

"Me, Kitty Boy, and Alex will drop in on the roof and rescue Gaymer and Joshua." Salvador moved to stand beside his team.

Putting an arm around Gato, Esmerelda said, "Freddy, Gato, and I will hold back until we're needed."

"You, Fire, Boots, and I will attack and draw out their foot soldiers," Aspen answered, transforming into Ice.

Transforming into Fire, Aiden asked, "Are we cannon fodder?"

"Yes," Chitter answered, pushing buttons on the console that caused the side of the box van to open, revealing the hover discs and a black satchel. "The satchel is for Boots. It's loaded with concussion bombs he can drop."

Fierce looked around. "Meow?"

"You're a kitten and shouldn't be in battle." Alex looked at the Mobile Shadow Command Center. "Maybe you can ride in the Mobile Shadow Command Center with Chitter and Alegro?"

Fierce jumped from Boots' arms. "Meow!"

"You can be our backup," Esmerelda said, kneeling down to scratch Fierce on the head.

Diego tapped his chest, activating his Shadow Guardian suit. "Did we leave enough Shadow Drones for Juan Carlos to patrol with?"

"We only brought the three standard Shadow Drones to carry the Boyfriend Brigade to the top of the laboratory," Chitter answered.

Alegro vibrated. Tapping buttons on his console, the top of the box van slid open, and three Shadow Drones flew out to hover in the air.

"Standard Shadow Drones?" Alex asked, tapping his wrist to activate his High Tech suit.

Freddy snickered. "I love that your suit is based on one of my old go-go boy outfits."

"You don't still have that outfit?" Salvador asked with a smile. "Do you?"

Red magic swirled around Freddy, transforming him into Lobo. With a growl in his voice, he said, "I might have an outfit or two."

"I'm not sure about being separated from Boots." Pink magic swirled around Keagan. Pink fur armor appeared, along with a tail and ears. "It feels weird."

Putting a hand on Kitty Boy's shoulder, Shadow Guardian said, "I'll protect Boots from harm on your behalf, and you protect High Tech in there for me."

"Agreed." Kitty Boy smiled at him.

Alegro vibrated. The three Shadow Drones lowered to ground level.

"Wait." High Tech stepped onto his. "You didn't answer my question about standard Shadow Drones."

Alegro vibrated.

"I know it's getting close to midnight, but you can tell me what you mean..." High Tech's voice was lost as he rose into the air.

Lobo stopped Salvador before he stepped onto his Shadow Drone. "Be safe."

"You too." He tapped his wrist, activating his Siren bodysuit decorated with white musical notes. He kissed Lobo on the nose, then stepped on his Shadow Drone. "The age of the Demon Twink is over."

Boots brought out his wings. He took Kitty Boy by the hand and pulled Kitty Boy toward him.

Boots dipped him, then kissed him passionately. "You be safe too."

"You too," Kitty Boy said when he righted himself. "Don't take any unnecessary risks."

Gato chuckled. "His cheeks are as pink as his fur."

"Meow," Fierce added merrily.

"Yeah. Yeah." Kitty Boy stepped onto his Shadow Drone. "Is this thing," the Shadow Drone rose up into the air, "safe?!"

Gaymer turned at the strange smell of cotton candy, candy canes, and birthday cake. Finn stood there, the smoke from his appearance fading away. Crossing his arms, Gaymer said, "You could have made it smell like that the entire time?"

"I guess so. I didn't think it would work." Finn shrugged. "It's time. Are you ready?"

Gaymer took the flash drive from his pocket, quickly inserted it into one of the ports on his computer, then opened the lone program with a skull and crossbones as an icon. All around him the computers started fizzing and popping as the screens went blank with tiny puffs of smoke.

Gaymer smiled at Finn. "I'm ready. Let's go."

"You're not going with me." Finn held up a hand to stop Gaymer from approaching. "Your rescuers are on their way." He smiled. "They just landed on the roof."

Confused, Gaymer asked, "Why don't you just take me from here?"

"Alas, we must make it look as though we were betrayed by Doctor Gingerman and you were rescued by the heroes." Finn shrugged. "Demon politics and such."

Stepping back, Gaymer asked, "Who is coming for me? Is it Ice? Is she here?"

"She's around but not with the ones coming for you." Finn took Gaymer's hand. "I really enjoyed our walks. If you ever wish to chat again," he tapped the charmed bracelet, "there are ways."

Worried, Gaymer grabbed Finn's hand before he could pull it away. "Are you going to be okay?"

"I am more resilient than you think." Finn pulled his hand away. "It's time to make them regret underestimating me." Finn stepped back and disappeared in a puff of smoke, leaving the scent of cotton candy, candy canes, and birthday cake behind.

Joshua stood at the horrific screams that came through the walls of his cell. He looked around for something to make into a weapon. The blood curdling screams stopped suddenly. Joshua swallowed. Nails came through the door that led to his cell. They pulled the door open.

"Death Drop?" Joshua laughed when he saw her. "Here I thought I was in danger."

Her eyes glowed red. Her smile was filled with sharp, jagged teeth. Joshua regretted his words when she lumbered forward, her hand out and fingers splayed with her dagger-sharp nails extended. She let out a crazed laugh. She swiped at the cell, slicing the bars and sending them tumbling to the ground.

Joshua grabbed the only thing available to him, his pillow, and threw it at her. It smacked her in the face. She stopped. Her eyes returned to normal. She looked down at the pillow, then at Joshua. She raised an eyebrow while scratching her head with her nails.

"It's all I had," Joshua answered the unspoken question.

Death Drop crossed her arms. Cocking her head left then right, she pointed at Joshua's boxer briefs.

"I have never been judged so harshly about my choice in underwear before." Joshua groaned. "Are you here to kill me? Annoy me? What?"

Death Drop wiggled her nails at Joshua. When she stepped closer, Joshua punched her in the face. She stopped and looked cross-eyed at her bent nose. She straightened it. She wiggled her nose. Then she put her hands on her hips and glared at Joshua. He punched her again, sending her stumbling back.

"Did you really think I wasn't going to fight back?" Joshua asked, prepared to strike again.

Death Drop hissed. She took a swipe at Joshua with her dagger nails. Putting his arms up in protection, Joshua closed his eyes and prepared himself for the attack. When it didn't come, he lowered his arms and opened his eyes. He was in a magical bubble with a confused Death Drop on the other side running her nails over the shield.

Joshua looked down at his medallion. It glowed on his chest. Joshua put his thumb in his ears and stuck his tongue out at Death Drop. "Ha ha. You can't get me."

Enraged, Death Drop repeatedly swiped at the protective bubble. She let out a howl of frustration.

"Betrayal." Death Drop turned at the sound of Lip-Sync's voice. "Really? That's so tacky." She did a fan kick that knocked Death Drop aside. "I taught you better."

Death Drop hissed. Raising her hand, she shot out several nails at Lip-Sync.

Lip-Sync clacked her fan open and knocked them away with a twist of her wrists. "I take it that you're no longer interested in being my protégé." Death Drop lunged at her. Lip-Sync brought her knee up in time, connecting with Death Drop's chin and sending her flying upward. Lip-Sync punched her in the gut, sending Death Drop flying back to land on her butt. "You're not up to my caliber."

Death Drop hissed. Black magic swirled around her and dripped up as she sank down. She pointed her two fingers at her eyes and then back at Lip-Sync.

"Yeah, I'm watching you too." Unimpressed, Lip-Sync crossed her arms and watched her disappear into the blackness. She turned to Joshua. She put a hand on the magical protection, and it lowered. Offering her hand, she said, "Come on. Let's get you out of here."

Taking her hand, Joshua asked, "What's going on? What happened out there?"

"The usual. Betrayal. Murder. The pretty heroine rescuing the gallant in distress," Lip-Sync teased. "Shall we go?"

Joshua pulled her close. He held up the necklace with his other hand. "You knew what this was, didn't you?"

"I did." Lip-Sync swallowed hard. "It was my father's. I thought I lost it when those men attacked me."

"Then you should have it back." Joshua began lifting it over his head.

Lip-Sync stopped him. "No, you keep it. He was a police officer who died in the line of duty. It's fitting that you have it." She smiled at him. "I put a protection spell into it when I saw it on you. As long as you wear it, I know you'll be safe."

"Lip-Sync, join us," Joshua pleaded. "You obviously have a good heart."

Lip-Sync shook her head. "There is very little good left in my heart." Before Joshua could counter, they were enveloped in a cloud of smoke.

CHAPTER 25

FIRE AND ICE FLANKED SHADOW
Guardian as they zoomed toward the labo-
ratory. Above them, Boots flew. Ahead of them,
Kitty Boy, Siren, and High Tech dropped down
onto the roof. Slowing the Shadow Disc, Shadow
Guardian gave the signal to start the attack.

Fire and Ice each raised an arm and blasted
the building with their powers. Alarms started
sounding as the wall began to crumble from the
concentrated heat and cold that hit it. Spotlights
illuminated the scene. Shadow Guardian signaled
Boots. He dove at the lights, knocking them out
with his concussion bombs.

"Boyfriend Brigade is in the building," Chitter
announced over the coms.

Muscle minions dressed from head to
toe in black came running from the building,

brandishing shock sticks and the same shock guns the Puppy Pack used in Morgan City a few weeks earlier. They scattered into the darkness, following the light from Ice's and Fire's attacks to their source.

"We've been spotted," Shadow Guardian announced. "Scatter."

Fire zoomed to the left, while Ice zoomed to the right. Shadow Guardian did a loop and did a run over the muscle minions, letting the Shadow Drone empty its inventory of Shadow Darts. Boots did the same, dropping concussion and smoke bombs into the mindless muscle minions.

The wall collapsed. Another wave of muscle minions came forth from the building. Behind the attacking heroes, the door to a hidden bunker opened. From it came yet another wave of muscle minions, blasting blindly into the night air. Behind them came several armored Jeeps with larger shock guns mounted on the back.

"Chitter," Shadow Guardian called, leaping from his Shadow Disc a moment before it was struck by a blast from an armored Jeep, "send in the Shadow Drones."

Boots zoomed by and caught Shadow Guardian by the ankles. "Sorry, I was going for your wrists," he apologized, flying over the battle below.

"Actually, this works perfectly." Shadow Guardian extended his arms and began spraying muscle minions with his Shadow Darts. "Do you think you can drop me on one of those Jeeps?"

Boots changed direction toward the Jeeps. "I'm great at dropping things. It's catching things I have problems with."

"Alex has that same problem." Shadow Guardian laughed.

Boots dropped Shadow Guardian. He activated his glider wings and angled himself at the unsuspecting Jeep. Tucking in his wings, he angled himself to kick the gunner of one of the Jeeps. Sending the man flying from the Jeep, he grabbed the gun and blasted the Jeep beside them, sending it flipping over.

He turned to aim at the other Jeep. When he did, Boots landed on the hood with so much force it crushed the front end and sent the occupants flying from the vehicle. Boots shot back up into the air to repeat the procedure on two more Jeeps.

"Show-off," Shadow Guardian grumbled. The Jeep he was on veered sharply to the left then right. He looked down to see the driver trying to get his weapon out to attack. Shadow Guardian quickly shot him with a Shadow Dart before leaping from the out of control Jeep.

Ice hurled down hailstones on the army of muscle minions, while Fire rained down blasts of fire. For every muscle minion they took out, three more appeared. They were quickly being outnumbered, and they couldn't keep up their attacks and dodge the shots from the shock weapons.

Fire sent several more blasts down at the growing number of muscle minions that poured out of the building. "Seriously, how many muscle minions do they have?"

"We need help over here," Ice said into the coms, biting down a curse. She dodged a blast. Fire hit the offending muscle minion in the chest, knocking him to the ground.

Alegro's robotic voice came over the coms. "Dragon Shadow Drones are incoming."

"Dragon Shadow Drones?" Fire questioned, dodging several shots from below.

Twenty-four dragon-shaped Shadow Drones strafed the battlefield with Shadow Darts. They circled back. This time, they shot tiny missiles from their wings. The missiles exploded over the muscle minions, releasing the electrified nets that incapacitated anyone that it touched.

Ice took a deep breath. "Time to cool things down." She whipped up the wind and lowered the temperature rapidly, freezing the ground below them. Snow and ice began swirling around, blinding the muscle minions.

"I think it's time to heat things up!" Taking advantage of the hindered muscle minions, Fire sent blast after blast at them.

An orange ball of energy hit both Fire and Ice, knocking them to the ground. "Aww, the elementals. I've been waiting for this rematch." Dante grinned viciously.

"Esmerelda! Gato! Lobo! Go!" Alegro ordered over the com.

From the woods, Lobo emerged. He knocked muscle minions to the side, clearing a path for the others. Riding atop a black panther, Esmerelda sent out concentrated blasts of magic to subdue groups of muscle minions. Gato raced beside her, pouncing and knocking away any they missed that were foolish enough to try to still attack.

Above them, the Dragon Shadow Drones spread out over the masses of muscle minions, strafing the ever-growing army. Carrying Shadow Guardian by the wrists, Boots flew ahead, dropping Shadow Guardian between Fire and Ice.

"So nice of you to join us." Ice quickly put up an ice dome to protect them. "We can't keep this up. They are overwhelming us by sheer numbers."

Fire flexed her fingers. "We need to take out the Demon Twink."

"Peek-a-boo! I see you!" Dante said a moment before shattering the ice dome with a magical blast. He sent another magical blast at the three. Before it struck, Boots landed in front of them and wrapped them in his wings. Dante hissed when the blast was absorbed harmlessly by Boots.

"A gargoyle! You're a gargoyle!" Annoyed, he pelted Boots with magical blasts. "I should have guessed, given your lineage." Dante disappeared in a puff of smoke, evading one of Esmerelda's magical attacks. He reappeared on top of the building. "For shame, Gitana. I would have thought you would have better aim than that."

Boots turned and began knocking muscle minions away with his wings. "What does he mean by my lineage?"

"We'll figure it out later," Ice said, creating giant snow drifts for the muscle minions to climb over.

Lobo howled. He, Esmeralda, and Gato were surrounded. "How many thralls does he have?" he growled, sending a group flying with a swipe of his paws.

"More than you can handle." Dante laughed from atop the roof. "Surrender now, and I'll make your deaths quick and painless."

Shadow Guardian called over the coms, "Chitter, get squirrely."

Holding his palm up to the control panel, High Tech said, "As expected, all the guards have been dispatched to deal with the others." He scanned the data that came across his visor. "It looks like Gaymer is two levels down. I can't find Joshua anywhere. I don't think he's here."

"Let's get him and get out of here, then," Kitty Boy said, tail whipping about anxiously. "This place gives me the creeps."

Siren asked, "Have they sent out The Three Bears?"

"No." High Tech pulled his hand from the console. "We can assume they are guarding Gaymer." He pointed to the stairwell. "Let's go."

Kitty Boy jumped his way down the stairs, followed by Siren and High Tech. Kitty Boy cautiously opened the door. Seeing no danger, he led the way onto the floor. High Tech pointed down the hall to the only illuminated door. It flickered as they approached.

"We've got to hurry. It's phasing out of this dimension," Siren announced.

The three made it with barely a second to spare, slamming into the Three Bears as they were trying to leave.

"You idiots!" Papa Bear shouted. "Now we're all trapped in here!"

Standing up, he grabbed Kitty Boy by the tail and hurled him across the room. Using his enhanced reflexes, Kitty Boy turned so when his feet hit the wall, and he kicked out, sending him flying back at Papa Bear. Mama Bear stood, blocking Kitty Boy's trajectory. He slammed into her hair, knocking Mama Bear off-balance and onto Papa Bear.

"What is it with you and my hair?!" Mama Bear shrieked. She tried to grab Kitty Boy by the feet, but he disappeared into her beehive. She flailed her arms, knocking Papa Bear about. "You filthy creature! Get out of my hair!"

Using the distraction, High Tech shot tendrils into Honey Bear's weaponry, reprogramming it, then pulling himself and Gaymer away from the Three Bears. "It's nice to finally meet you," he said to Gaymer as they stood. "Stay behind us."

"They sent a go-go boy to rescue me?" Gaymer asked, bewildered. "And why is he pink?"

Kitty Boy poked his head out the top of Mama Bear's wig. "I like pink."

Dumbfounded, Gaymer said, "Keagan?"

"Get over here," Siren ordered.

Kitty Boy ducked down into Mama Bear's beehive, then came flying out to land beside the others. "Hey, Gaymer, long time no see."

"You're pink and furry." Gaymer tentatively touched his arm.

Keagan growled. "Yeah, a lot has happened while you were gone."

"Look! I have four new little toys!" Honey Bear raised his hand to send out blasts, but instead, his gun exploded, trapping the Three Bears in the honey amber goo.

Struggling to break free, Papa Bear lamented, "Not again!"

"Oh, you are very bad boys!" Mama Bear growled. "Not only did you ruin my hair, but you ruined my outfit!"

High Tech put a hand on Siren's shoulder. "How about getting us out of here so we can help out our boyfriends?"

"Gladly." Siren sang an A-flat, opening a portal for them. "We'll be back for you," he said before stepping through the portal with the others.

Finn barged into Doctor Gingerman's office. "Why aren't The Three Bears out there helping Dante?!"

"Because he doesn't deserve my help." Doctor Gingerman yawned. "This partnership is over."

Finn's eyes glowed red. "I knew we couldn't trust you."

"Oh, no. The lackey is mad." Doctor Gingerman laughed. "Whatever should I do?" He snapped his fingers. Death Drop appeared. "She may not have brought me Sentry, but she did dispatch everyone in that forgotten Hell dimension you were hiding him in."

Delighted with herself, Death Drop cackled.

Finn formed a ball of red magic. "You both will pay for your betrayal."

"I think it's about time you got better acquainted with the Head of the Board." Doctor Gingerman picked up the white dog, holding it out. "She thinks you're a tasty snack."

The white dog's hair shot out toward Finn. Thinking fast, he used his power to yank Death Drop in front of him to block the mystical dog's attack. Death Drop tried to break free, but the hair wrapped tighter and tighter around her until she was wrapped from head to toe in it. When the hair retreated a moment later, there was nothing left of her.

"Oh well, she was annoying." Doctor Gingerman patted the head of the mystical dog. "Your turn."

Finn shot a blast at the dog, but it opened its mouth and swallowed the shot easily. "What is it?"

"Something older than you or I." Doctor Gingerman held the dog out again. This time, when the dog's hair shot out, Finn disappeared in a puff of smoke before it could get a hold of him. The alarm sounded on Doctor Gingerman's watch. "It looks as if all of our henchmen have failed us."

Tucking the creature under his arm, Doctor Gingerman grabbed a crystal from his desk and slammed it into the ground in front of him. A portal back to his penthouse appeared. "Well, we have other options available to us, don't we?" He kissed the creature on the head before stepping through.

CHAPTER 26

"G ET SQUIRRELY?" HIGH TECH asked, stepping through the portal and immediately jumping into battle. "I told you no squirrel army."

Chitter gleefully responded, "You didn't say we couldn't have an air force."

"Ice!" Gaymer rushed and hugged her. "You got the message from Finn! Is Chitter safe?"

Ice put an arm around him. "They are." She sent out an arctic chill, freezing several nearby muscle minions. "Us on the other hand? That's a different story."

"Boots!" Kitty Boy hugged him. He purred as he smacked away several muscle minions with his tail.

Boots smiled. "I like it when you purr."

"Weren't you guys supposed to have this all wrapped up by the time we got out?" Siren asked. He sang a quick harmony to block a blast from Dante.

Fire shot several blasts at Dante. "Things got complicated." She put up a wall of fire to ward off a group of charging muscle minions. "Where is Joshua?"

"He wasn't in there," High Tech answered, sending several shock balls out into the attacking forces.

"This is turning out better than expected." Dante blocked Fire's blasts. "All of my enemies vanquished in one night!" He laughed. "This wasn't even the plan!"

The ground shook, and everyone fell silent when a roaring "Meow" filled the air. All eyes turned to the booming steps of something large coming through the woods.

"He did say he was a lot bigger and more powerful than he appeared," Gato commented with a smile when he saw a ten-foot tall Fierce step out of the woods with Joshua on his back.

"Did anyone order a squadron of flying squirrels?" Joshua asked, waving from Fierce's back.

Above him, the stars were blocked by dozens of tiny black squares. When they were over their targets, they tucked in their flaps to dive bomb, then opened their flaps to buzz over the muscle minions' heads, releasing their payloads of concussion acorns.

"Meow!" Fierce ran forward, swatting any unfortunate muscle minions that crossed his path out of the way.

Dante raised a hand to blast Fierce. "Bad kitty!"

Before Dante could release his blast, the building shook. Behind him, the laboratory erupted in rubble and fire. Finn appeared by his side to steady him. Finn extended a hand. The muscle minions sank down into pools of black magic.

"Doctor Gingerman's betrayal is greater than we imagined," Finn explained. "We need to leave. Now!" Dante screamed in pain from a flying rod of rebar puncturing the back of his right shoulder.

Finn gripped the part that protruded from his front. "Brace yourself." The rebar sticking out of Dante's back fell to the ground. When it did, Finn yanked the remains through Dante's shoulder. Tossing the offending metal aside, he put a hand on Dante's wound to heal it.

"Thank you, my love." Dante allowed Finn to lift him to his feet. Below, the heroes were circling together as they evaded the erupting ground. "The explosions are disrupting the lines of magic.

I can't get us out of here. I'm afraid Doctor Gingerman won."

Finn looked down at the doomed heroes. "Not yet. Danger makes strange bedfellows." In a puff of smoke, they were gone from the rooftop, only to reappear in the center of the startled heroes. Drawing on Dante's power, Finn raised his free hand to the sky and sent red magic up, creating a red bubble around all of them. He shouted to the others, "Help me!"

"Gato, your hand." Esmerelda held her hand out, and Gato put his hand in hers. Joining their magic, Esmerelda held her hand out, adding their magic to the Demon Twinks.

Siren took Freddy's hand and did the same. "It's not enough," Siren said through gritted teeth.

"Boots." Kitty Boy took his hand. "We can help them." Together, they held their joined hands up, adding their power to the rest.

A normal sized Fierce jumped onto their arms. "Meow!" He put a paw on top of their joined hands and added his magic.

The magical bubble rose in the night sky as explosions illuminated the ground around them. Chitter and Alegro moved alongside them before taking the lead and guiding them back to the transformed box truck. Below them, the ground fell in as the explosions continued, obliterating the laboratory.

Landing safely at the truck, Chitter bounded out of the Mobile Shadow Command Center to jump into Gaymer's outstretched arms. "Gaymer!"

"Chitter!" Gaymer hugged them close. "I've missed you! Have you been a good squirrel?"

Ice put a hand on Gaymer's shoulder. "The best."

"Don't tell me you wore those on your date!" Fire yelled at Joshua before hugging him. "Are you okay?"

Joshua returned the hug. "Yes, I'm fine, and I'll get rid of these boxer briefs when we get home."

"I guess it's time to deal with these two," Lobo snarled, looming over the Demon Twinks.

Setting Chitter down, Gaymer rushed to block Lobo. "No. Finn did a kindness for me, and now I'm doing a kindness for him." He looked back at Finn, holding Dante up. "Let them go."

"Let them go." Esmerelda came up beside Freddy. The muscle in her jaw tightened when she addressed the Demon Twinks. "This is your one mercy by us."

Finn put a hand on Gaymer's shoulder. "Thank you."

"Tell me, Gitana, whose side will you take," Dante laughed as smoke began to swirl around them, "in the Demon Wars?"

Shadow Guardian put a hand on Esmerelda's shoulder. "Let's get home. It's been a long night."

CHAPTER 27

DOUG TRAINER STIRRED. OPENING his eyes, he smiled. There was no moon tonight, but the city cast enough light for him to make out Brutus' silhouette in front of the barred window of his hospital room. It warmed his heart to know that he had this time, though minute, with Brutus.

He patted the bed. "Come sit with me. Tell me what troubles you."

"This place is nothing more than a cage, keeping us from running free." Brutus turned from the window. He took in a deep breath then exhaled it. "I'm sorry." He sat down on the bed. Carefully, he picked up Doug's hand and set it in his lap. "We shouldn't be here. We should be out there, ruling this city."

Doug shook his head. "We are where we are supposed to be. In the morning, I'll have the first of my surgeries to repair my hands, and we'll stand trial. Then we'll help get Gaymer back however we can."

"There will be no surgery or trial," Brutus proclaimed. "We will not help those who put us here."

Doug shook his head. "Brutus, you're speaking nonsense. They'll be here in a couple of hours to prep me for surgery."

"There will be no surgery," Brutus reaffirmed. He looked at his lover. "You once promised me that you'd never let me be locked in a cage again."

Doug felt the guilt from breaking that promise. "If only I could have kept that promise."

"I made the same promise to you," Brutus said, his voice determined. "I intend to keep that promise."

Doug's voice broke when he spoke. "Brutus, what did you do?"

"What I had to," Brutus answered.

Doug raised his voice. "Brutus, what did you do?!"

"I made a deal," Brutus answered calmly. "We made a deal."

Doug shook his head in disbelief. "Tell me you didn't." Louder, he repeated it, this time an order. "Tell me you didn't!"

"It fell upon me to lead our Pack when you were taken away from us." Brutus' voice didn't waver when he spoke. "We were humiliated—defeated by Juan Carlos and those Lunarray Wolves. We would have won had they not interfered. They will pay for besmirching our victory."

Angrily, Doug repeated, "What did you do?!"

"I made a deal." Brutus' eyes flared red with fire.

Doug shook his head and tried to pull his hand back. Fear filled his voice. "No, Brutus, you didn't! Tell me you didn't! The Demon Twink cannot be trusted!"

"The Demon Twink couldn't be trusted, but the Gingerman can be." The flames swirled in Brutus' eyes. "He has given us power unlike any that filthy Demon Twink ever could." The shackles fell off Brutus, and his orange jumpsuit burned away to show him in a bulldog harness and black skintight pants. "I now lead the Demon Hounds."

Fearful, Doug yanked his hand away. "No, Brutus."

"Yes." The word echoed in the room. The building shook. Car alarms below started going off. The lights in the hospital flickered. He took Doug's hand. "A gift to show you my love."

Black magic swirled around their hands. Doug screamed in agony as the bones and muscles mended. When Doug tried to break Brutus' grip with his other hand, it too was caught up in the magic.

There was pounding on the door. Doug's screams ended when he passed out from the pain. Brutus released his hands. Ignoring the shouts from the guards and nurses, Brutus stood and gathered Doug into his arms.

"Come, my love." Brutus smiled down at his lover. "Our pack awaits."

Brutus let out an ear-piercing howl that shattered the glass around them. A black circle of magic formed below them. He kissed his lover on the forehead as they sank into the black portal.

"You seriously wore those on your date?" Gaymer asked Joshua, trying not to laugh.

Joshua groaned. "I didn't expect anyone to see them, especially after I accidently stabbed the waiter."

Gaymer's eyes went big. "You accidently stabbed the waiter?"

"Yup." Joshua's cheeks flushed pink. "The same one that Diego traumatized last year."

Alex shook his head, covering his mouth to hide his laughter. "That poor waiter."

"I'll pay for his therapy." Diego groaned, putting an arm around Alex.

Pulling Gaymer closer to him, Aspen asked, "Other than the poor choice in underwear, traumatizing the wait staff, and being kidnapped, how was your date?"

"Oddly good. We talked while we walked. She transformed into a mouse to help me battle Death Drop." Joshua laughed, remembering Death Drop trapped under the chandelier. "She brought me a chicken fingers basket from In Between, so I knew she passed the word on to you guys, and she gave me a piece of cake with a file in it." Joshua paused. "The file!" He pulled the flash drive from his underwear. "What do you think is on here?"

Keagan raised an eyebrow. "Besides you?"

"Where else was I going to hide it?" Joshua asked. "Anyway, she then came to my rescue, defeated Death Drop, then brought me to the truck and Fierce. Then we came to save the day." He idly played with the medallion around his neck. "Turns out this necklace Teddy and Jack gave to me was her father's. I wonder how they got it."

Esmerelda tapped a finger to her chin. "Odd bonds are being made." She pointed to Joshua. "You and Lip-Sync." She pointed to Gaymer. "You and Finn." She pointed at Boots. "You are still an anomaly, but you, Keagan, and Fierce."

"Meow." Fierce yawned curling up in Boots' lap.

Boots smiled. "That's right. I'm special."

"Change of subject," Gaymer spoke up. "We're all okay with Chitter driving this truck? And where did he get that ballcap and jean vest?"

Aiden raised his hand. "Yes. And I made them for him along with a bunch of other outfits."

"We'll have to find a place to live when we get back." Gaymer sighed. "I also have to get a job."

Aspen kissed Gaymer on the cheek. "You can stay with me, and if you're not comfortable with that, I'm sure Diego can find you someplace to stay in DJC Tower."

"As for work, consider this a formal job offer to work at JCA," Alex added.

Diego cocked his head at Alex. "You can do that?"

"What do you think the A in JCA stands for?" Alex asked with a wink.

Gaymer smiled. "A place to stay and a job. It looks like I'm set."

"What do you think the Demon Twink meant by whose side we will take in the Demon Wars?" Freddy asked.

Salvador patted his leg. "Correction: he asked Esmerelda whose side she'd take."

"I guess we'll see." Gato took Esmerelda's hand and kissed it. "We'll be by your side no matter what side you choose."

"Herc!" Demona shouted. "We have more coming in!"

Ryuu pushed his way through the growing masses of demon refugees. "Demona! I have room for three more fire demons in my cave!"

"Demona, the sanctuary pocket dimensions are at capacity," Herc shouted over the crowd.

Demona climbed up on a table. She sent a pulse of magic out to quiet the growing masses and get their attention. "Everyone, please be patient. It will be a few hours, but I have made arrangements for additional sanctuary dimensions."

"I just got word from Juan Carlos," Dion said, looking at her tablet. "The team is on their way back." She scanned her tablet before handing it up to Demona. "I think these are possible candidates for the relocation."

Demona scanned the screen. "This looks okay to me." She looked up at a red fireball flying into the bar. It paused and hovered next to Dion. "Hello, Mother."

"Hello, daughter." The fireball transformed into Hedan. Smiling at Dion, she said, "Dion, so nice to see you again. I wish it were under better circumstances."

Demona crossed her arms. "What is it, Mother? I'm busy here. In case you didn't notice, there's a Demon War going on."

"I know." Hedan took Dion's hand and reached up to take Demona's. "It pains me to ask this, but I formally request sanctuary." Demona jumped down from the table. "There isn't a Hell dimension not embroiled in war. Demon Hounds are raiding them all, devouring the weak and enslaving any that won't pledge their fealty to the Gingerman."

Demona hugged her mother. "Granted."

A portal opened. Three young imps came running through. Lip-Sync soon followed, closing the portal as she dove through it. She rolled into a standing position in front of the scared imps.

Smiling at Demona, Lip-Sync said, "Don't mind me. I thought I'd pop by and found these little ones in need of a ride." She motioned to the three imps hiding behind her. "I hope you have room for more."

"You're safe here." Dion stepped forward. "Let me get you something to eat and drink."

They reluctantly let Dion usher them away. When they were out of earshot, Demona asked, "What do you think you're doing, Lip-Sync?"

"I'm being the hero for them." Lip-Sync motioned to the three imps that she brought. "The one that no one else will be." She opened a portal and was off again.

CHAPTER 28

DANTE WOKE WITH A START IN HIS bed. Finn put a calming hand on his shoulder. "We're safe." Dante settled back down with a grimace. "Gingerman has declared war on all of the Hell dimensions. In Between has been overrun with refugees."

"Have our generals gather supplies to send to them." Dante put a hand over his mending wound. "Send in our forces to reinforce the lower dimensions."

Finn brushed away the hair from Dante's face. "Already done." He kissed Dante's forehead. "Our forces have swelled with recruits. The muscle minions are safe and recovering."

"It looks as though you thought of everything. I knew you were the perfect match for me." Dante brought Finn down for a kiss. "Is there anything I'm not thinking of that I should be asking?"

Finn laughed. "That is everything so far. I do have a surprise for you," he said and winked. He moved to a covered box. "I got us some pets." He pulled the sheet off the box, revealing an intricate hamster cage with a wheel, several climbing tubes, and three tiny little houses.

"Finn," Dante groaned, sitting up. He narrowed his eyes at the three tiny bodies pounding on the Plexiglas. He laughed in delight. "You delightful devil!"

Finn crouched down to look at The Three Bears futilely shouting. "I went back to survey the damage. The pocket dimension was still intact but slowly collapsing. That's where I found these three encased in that icky goo the tiny one shoots."

Finn returned his attention to Dante. "It would have been cruel to leave them there." He smiled wickedly. "It was crueler to shrink them down and put them in this terrarium."

"I love you." Dante chuckled. "I assume there's room for Gingerman in there?"

A chill ran down Finn's spine. "That dog of his is not natural and nothing I've ever seen before."

"That creature is one that hasn't been seen since time started." Dante sat up in the bed.

Finn put his arms around himself. "It ate Death Drop."

"It'll devour us all if we don't find a way to stop it." Dante held out his arms. "That is a tomorrow problem." Finn carefully rested his head against Dante's chest. "Today, we celebrate that we are alive."

Yawning and stretching, Keagan stepped out of the room with Boots at Diego and Alex's apartment. "Tonight, we sleep in our own apartment without any guests."

"What time is it?" Boots asked, scratching his head.

"Noon," Juan Carlos announced, popping around the corner holding Fierce. Keagan jumped up into the air and landed in Boots' arms. Juan Carlos coughed to cover his laugh. "There's food, juice, and coffee on the table. You better hurry before Joshua eats it all."

Joshua raised an eyebrow at Boots carrying Keagan into the dining room. Keagan looked at Boots carrying him. "Put me down."

"You two are too cute!" Aiden laughed, popping a forkful of scrambled eggs into his mouth.

Boots set Keagan down. "Where's everyone else?"

"Aspen and Gaymer will be up in a minute," Joshua answered, snatching a piece of toast. "They are in Shadow Command with that drive Lip-Sync gave me."

Sitting down, Keagan made a face. "Hopefully, they disinfected it."

"Yes, and I threw away the smiling face boxer shorts." Joshua passed the plate of scrambled eggs over to Boots. "I wonder what is on it."

Taking the plate, Boots asked, "Do you think you're going to see her again?"

"Absolutely not!" Juan Carlos pronounced, taking a seat at the table. "You both are lucky I don't give you a good talking to."

Felipe strolled in, carrying a package. "This was downstairs for Joshua." Handing it over, he took a seat beside his father. "I'm glad to see everyone is alive."

"I'm glad to see you're alive too!" Boots beamed back.

Confused, Felipe said, "Thank you?"

"Who is it from?" Aiden asked, looking over at the package.

Joshua flipped the box around. "It doesn't say." He tore open the packaging.

"What is it?" Aiden asked, leaning his head over.

Joshua pushed Aiden's head back. Opening the package, he stared down in confusion. Holding them up, he said, "Happy face boxer briefs?"

"There's a note." Aiden snatched it before Joshua could. "Don't wear these on our next date." He grinned at Joshua. "I wonder who it is from."

Joshua snatched the note from Aiden. "Shut it."

A tired Esmerelda, Freddy, Gato, and Salvador arrived. Freddy sniffed the air. Juan Carlos motioned for them to sit. Freddy rushed the table. Salvador laughed softly, taking a seat beside him.

"Thank you for letting us stay in your apartment last night." Esmerelda sat down in the chair Gato held out for her. "Thank you, dear."

Gato stretched then sat down. He looked at the underwear in Joshua's box. "You bought another pair?"

"His not so secret demon assassin admirer sent them to him," Aiden teased.

A portal opened. Demona stepped through. "Okay, gang. I am at capacity." She raised an eyebrow at the perplexed looks. "Refugees. From the Demon War that started last night." She looked around the table. "Diego and Alex arranged for this place to handle the overflow. I have twenty demons in need of a place to stay."

"They did what and you have what?" Juan Carlos asked, holding back his anger.

Demona held up a placating hand. "Dion handpicked them, and my mother will be keeping them in line."

"I need to have a word with Diego." Juan Carlos looked around. "Where is he by the way? He and Alex weren't in their bedroom this morning." Gaymer and Aspen came into the room looking pensive. Juan Carlos motioned for them to sit. "Get something to eat. We have company coming."

Aspen nudged Gaymer. Gaymer bit his lower lip. "I went through the data that was on the flash drive. It has information on all of Doctor Gingerman's dark experiments." He turned the tablet around in his hands. "It also has the genetic source material he used for Boots." Gaymer looked over at him. "I guess you could say we know who your parents are? I mean, we still have to verify that with blood tests, but according to the information, we know who they are."

"Who is it?" Juan Carlos asked curiously. "Who are Boots' parents?"

Gaymer looked at Aspen before handing the tablet over to Boots. "Read for yourself."

"Really?" Boots said after reading the information.

Keagan looked over at the tablet. "That makes total sense given how this week has been going, and from what I've seen, it checks out."

"Who is it?" Juan Carlos asked, annoyed. Boots handed over the tablet. Reading the information, he set the tablet down, then smacked Felipe in the back of the head.

Rubbing his head, Felipe asked, "What was that for?"

"Diego and Alex have given me two grand-children, and you haven't given me any!" Juan Carlos smiled over at Boots. "Welcome to the family, Boots."

Alegro zipped across the table to wrap around Boots, who laughed as Alegro vibrated. "Yes, you can be the big sibling." Boots laughed. "Yes, we can go flying sometime."

"Where are those two? I want to see the look on their faces when they find out they have another child out of wedlock." Juan Carlos shouted, "Alex! Diego!"

Alegro vibrated.

"Yeah, they left early this morning before everyone was awake." Chitter twitched his whiskers at Juan Carlos when he saw the stunned expression on his face. "Is that a problem? They said they'd be back today. He told us not to say anything unless someone asked."

"Oh dear." Esmerelda set her coffee down.

Freddy dropped his fork onto his plate. "His parents?"

"He knows." Juan Carlos hugged Chitter and Fierce tight.

Felipe asked, "Knows what?"

Alex sat with Diego on the grass, holding his hand. "Thank you for bringing me here."

"I wanted you to meet them," Diego said, a tear running down his cheek. "I have to thank Juan Carlos for getting them such a nice headstone."

Alex squeezed his hand. "It is nice." He reached over and brushed a tear from Diego's cheek. "Just because they aren't here with us physically doesn't mean they aren't here with us."

"I know." Diego moved his arm to put it around Alex. "It's not the same."

The wind blew. The sweet scent of flowers filled the air. Alex asked the obvious: "Juan Carlos doesn't know that you know, does he?"

"I'm certain that he knows by now that I know." Diego let out a humorless laugh. "This is why he told me never to speak ill of my parents. I wish I had a sign that they were proud of me."

The wind blew again. "Look." Alex pointed at the spot in front of the headstone. Colorful wildflowers began sprouting up in the shape of a heart. From the center, a single white carnation with a red center bloomed. Alex put an arm around Diego. "I think you got your sign."

EPILOGUE

MADAM ZELDA SAT IN HER CHAIR sipping her tea. She smiled, content with herself for passing the spirits' message on to their son. Setting her tea down, she used her cane to get up from the chair. She hobbled over to the window to gaze into the infinite that she lived in now.

"I told you!" Madam Zelda laughed. "Oh, come on out, you two. I know you're there."

Behind her, two bodies manifested: Destiny, wearing a wedding dress with splatters of mud across it, and Fate, wearing a pristine football uniform in black-and-white with a baseball helmet under their arm. They looked at each other, then stepped forward to stand beside Madam Zelda. Fate stood on her left and Destiny on her right.

"The lines are still clouded for us," Destiny said, their voice neutral as always.

In the same neutral voice, Fate added, "That creature was never meant to be freed from its prison. None of the other celestials know how it could have escaped."

"So they do not believe it has," Madam Zelda stated bluntly. "That is the problem with you all-knowing beings. If you don't know it, then you don't believe it is."

Fate cocked their head at her. "We are all knowing. We would know if that creature escaped."

"Yet the creature is there," Madam Zelda argued. "Somehow it has clouded all of your visions."

Destiny looked at her. "That is not possible."

"Tell me what you see along the lines of fate and destiny, then," Madam Zelda challenged.

Fate's and Destiny's eyes changed to show the universe spinning in their eyes. Fate blinked. They frowned. Destiny blinked, then tried again. Both finally gave up, a perplexed look crossing their faces.

"You can't, can you?" Madam Zelda sighed.

A slight hint of annoyance edged into Destiny's voice. "We will yield to your wisdom."

"Walk your path lightly," Fate warned. "The other celestials are not as lenient as we are."

Madam Zelda stomped her cane. "Tell them if they were doing their job properly, I wouldn't be cleaning up their mess. I will do what I need to. Now go. I'm expecting company."

Fate and Destiny looked forward. In unison, they said, "We will pass the message." They stepped back and then faded away.

Beside her, a white light swirled, turning into a handsome young man with short black hair combed to the side, dressed in a tight black V-neck short-sleeved shirt and jeans. He smirked at Madam Zelda in the reflection.

"Don't you look spry," Madam Zelda teased. "You just missed Fate and Destiny."

He laughed. "That's the way I timed it."

"It would be a lot easier to deal with them if all-knowing beings accepted the fact that they are not all knowing." Madam Zelda turned and returned to her chair.

The man turned and dropped down to one knee before her. "My dear, you do the work of deities. I, Father Time, am humbled to be in your presence."

"Your words are slicker than oil." Madam Zelda laughed. She extended her hand. "Now, where are you taking me on our date?"

Standing, he kissed her hand. "Where? Spain." He winked at her. "As for when, I believe you said you'd like to meet some knight errant?"

RECIPE

CROQUETAS, ALSO KNOWN AS CRO-quettes in English.

Diego brought croquetas to In Between as a peace offering. Croquetas are a wonderful cheap thing to make that people go wild over. They aren't hard to make, but it takes time to make them. When you eat them, it's like you're tasting home. That is how I feel when I eat them. Hot or cold, I love them. They never really taste the same every time you make them because you're using leftover chicken that was seasoned from the previous meal, but when you bite into them, you taste that love that was used to make them.

Normally, my mother only made croquetas maybe twice a year. My mother grew up in Spain under the rule of the Fascist dictator Francisco Franco. That meant she grew up learning how to make food stretch. One way she learned to stretch food was croquetas. They were always made with leftover chicken or turkey.

When I am talking about leftover chicken or turkey, I'm talking about a whole chicken or turkey after a meal and all the big portions of meat are cut off the bird. She'd take the carcass and pull off all the little bits of meat that stuck to the bones. Then she'd toss the bones into a big ole pot and make stock.

My mother's recipe is a bit different from what you'd find out there. Trust me, I know. I showed her a recipe I found, and she made a face that can only be described as disgust when she saw the ingredients. Then she taught me how to make them her way. That being said, this is her recipe and not the one you'll find in cookbooks or on the internet.

What you'll need:

- Shredded chicken (any meat can be substituted)
- Onion (optional)
- Parsley
- Chicken stock
- Flour
- Eggs

- Italian Bread Crumbs
- Oil
- Frying pan dough
- Frying pan for frying
- Rubber spatulas
- Salt
- Pepper
- Someone to keep Bonita away from the chicken.

If you noticed, there are no measurements. The reason is because when you make croquetas, it's always leftover chicken. This is also why you only have the salt and pepper seasoning. The chicken should already be seasoned from your previous meal. If you made chicken solely to make croquetas, then season appropriately. Don't go overboard. At most, I'll add more salt and pepper to the shredded chicken, which is the only reason it's in the ingredients list.

If you use onion, I suggest adding a small amount of onion, minced finely. Put it in the frying pan and sweat it. Some people add it to the chicken. Either way is fine. Depending on how you did the onion, if you used the onion, add the chicken to the frying pan over medium heat. Once the chicken is reheated, add a spoonful of flour and stir it into the chicken. I use a rubber spatula because it's easier.

Of course, the flour is going to soak up all the moisture, so add a little chicken stock. Add parsley. Why? I don't know. My mother told me I had to, so I do. That'll be the only time you add the parsley. The rest is flour. Stir. Chicken stock. Stir. Repeat until you have a meat dough. This is why there aren't any measurements, because you have to eyeball it.

When you're ready, you transfer the dough to a plate to rest and cool. I normally put mine in the refrigerator and wait. This gives you time to clean up your mess because you'll have gotten flour all over your stove.

When the dough is rested, you beat 2–3 eggs in a bowl. I pour a little almond milk in mine. Pour Italian bread crumbs into a bag, turn on your favorite show, grab the dough and another plate, sit down, and begin forming the croquetas. Make sure you're comfortable.

Using a spoon, you'll slice into the dough and make ovals no bigger than an inch thick. Then dredge them in the egg, and finally, put them in the bag of Italian bread crumbs to coat them. Set them aside. Personally, I recommend doing the ovals then doing the dredging, but that's up to you as long as it's done.

You're going to let them rest while you heat up oil. If you're using a deep fryer, you can do that. I personally use a deep frying pan with about an inch of oil. You want to heat the oil to 350 degrees. When the oil is hot enough, add the breaded meat dough. Don't crowd them. Give them room to cook.

It only takes about a minute or so before you turn them. After another minute, pull them from the oil and set them on a paper towel. You want them golden brown. Check your oil temperature and repeat. That's it. Let them cool and serve. No sauces are needed. Any not eaten can be refrigerated for a couple of days or until they're gone. Whichever comes first.

Again, this is my mother's recipe so it is different from what you see out there saying you need nutmeg or milk. Those aren't wrong. Okay, they are wrong because my mother's recipe is the best, and you can't tell me otherwise. Enjoy!

BOOK CLUB QUESTIONS

1. Do you think Finn Andrews truly considers Gaymer a friend, or is he a means to an end?

2. Do you think Joshua Waters had an influence on Lip-Sync, or did he bring out something in her that was already there?

3. Esmerelda was ready to vanquish Boots the moment she saw him because she sensed he was a demon. Herc and Ryuu disliked him as well. Does this mean all demons are evil? If so, does that make Demona half evil?

4. Keagan and Boots are fated lovers, but no one is allowed to tell them that. What is your take on fated lovers?

5. Why do you think Keagan is shy with Boots? Is it his body or that he is attracted to him?

6. Alex comes up with a program to allow Alegro to communicate directly with everyone. Alex says he knows it made Alegro feel like an outsider not being able to directly communicate with everyone. Do you think this is the case?

7. If you were Joshua, would you have gone out on that date with Lip-Sync?

8. Esmerelda sees great evil in Boots. Salvador sees great good in Boots. Are they seeing what they want?

9. Why do you think Alex is reluctant to fully move in with Diego?

10. When Diego takes Alex to see his parents, he wishes he had some sort of sign that they were proud of him. Given that Juan Carlos took him in and raised him, why do you think he wanted to know they were proud of him?

AUTHOR BIO

ROBERT (ROBBY) J. LEWIS IS A writer based out of Charleston, South Carolina. He has brought you not only the Shadow Guardian series but the Someone Series under Robert Lewis. He has written numerous steamy film scripts for Noir Male and Icon Male and more recently agreed to start writing for Luxxxe Studios. You can keep up with Robby Lewis's latest releases, news, and antics via his social media or at www.robert-j-lewis.com.

Discover more at
4HorsemenPublications.com

10% off using HORSEMEN10